ARCHIE GOES HOME

ALSO BY ROBERT GOLDSBOROUGH

ARCHIE GOES HOME

A Nero Wolfe Mystery

Robert Goldsborough

MYSTERIOUSPRESS.COM

OPEN ROAD

INTEGRATED MEDIA

NEW YORK

All rights reserved, including without limitation the right to reproduce this book or any portion thereof in any form or by any means, whether electronic or mechanical, now known or hereinafter invented, without the express written permission of the publisher.

This is a work of fiction. Names, characters, places, events, and incidents either are the product of the author's imagination or are used fictitiously. Any resemblance to actual persons, living or dead, businesses, companies, events, or locales is entirely coincidental.

Copyright © 2020 by Robert Goldsborough

Cover design by Ian Koviak

978-1-5040-5988-6

Published in 2020 by MysteriousPress.com/Open Road Integrated Media, Inc.
180 Maiden Lane
New York, NY 10038

To John O'Loughlin

for his constant

enthusiasm and encouragement

ARCHIE GOES HOME

CHAPTER 1

This all began innocently, although I have been around long enough to be suspicious of what seems to be an innocuous telephone call like the one I received on a sunny June morning as I sat in the office with coffee after breakfast. The voice at the other end belonged to my aunt Edna, who was phoning from down in southern Ohio, the area where I was born and reared.

Edna usually calls when she's concerned about my mother, which has gotten to be a little more frequently the last few years. "Is it about Mom?" I asked, clenching the receiver as if I were trying to strangle it.

"Oh, well, she is . . . all right, Archie, she is just fine," my aunt said without conviction. "And please don't tell her that I telephoned you. I have enough of a reputation as a busybody as it is."

"Then what is the problem?" I learned long ago that you don't rush Edna Wainwright, my mother's slightly younger sister. She is going to tell a story at her own pace, and there is nothing anyone can do to speed her up. Maybe that's because of where she lives. Everything in that hilly, semirural region down near the Ohio River moves at a pace New Yorkers would call excruciatingly slow. I leaned back in my desk chair and drained the last of Fritz Brenner's fine brew from my cup. The sweep second hand on my watch had nearly made a full revolution when Aunt Edna cleared her throat. Progress.

"I am sure that you must remember Logan Mulgrew."

"How could I forget him, even after all the years I've been away," I said. "He has run the Farmer's State Bank & Trust since long before I snuck out of town and headed to New York lo those many eons ago."

"He doesn't run it anymore, Archie. He was found dead at home three days ago."

"Hardly a surprise. He must have been close to eighty, wasn't he?"

"Eighty-four, to be exact. But he did not die of natural causes," Aunt Edna said. "When he had not shown up at the bank for two days, his grandniece got worried and went to his house—you know, that big old pile of brick and stone south of town out on the Portsmouth Road, not far from where your mother lives."

"I remember the house well; it was the largest place around by far, wasn't it?"

"And without doubt the gloomiest," she said. "Logan had lived there alone ever since his wife, Sylvia, died early last year. And they never had any children. Anyway, when Donna Newman, that's the grandniece, went into the house, she found her uncle dead on the sofa in the living room, with a hole in his temple and a pistol lying on the seat cushion next to his outstretched hand. He had been dead for some time."

"Suicide," I said.

"Not likely," Aunt Edna replied in a tone that defied contradiction. "I probably knew Logan as well as almost anyone in the area, and he was not a man to take his own life, that much I can say."

"He probably found out that he had a terminal illness, and he didn't want to—"

"No, Archie, no," my aunt interrupted. "His grandniece said he recently had a checkup, and the physician found him so fit that he could have passed for a man at least fifteen years younger."

"What do the police think?"

"The police—that would be our young chief, Tom Blankenship—has said the doctor who examined the body found nothing to indicate anything suspicious in the way of a disease."

"What is your opinion of this Blankenship?"

"Oh, he's all right, I suppose," Edna said dismissively. "He has been on the job for five . . . well, almost six years now, and there really hasn't been much crime around here, unless you count a car chase after a holdup in which a couple of shots got fired, which fortunately didn't hit anybody. This isn't like New York, you know, where violence is just a way of life."

"It really is not that bad," I told her, but I was not about to press the point. I knew the image that small-town America—Aunt Edna included—has of New York and other large cities, while exaggerated, contains some merit. "So what do you plan to do about Mr. Mulgrew's death?"

"It has been quite a while since you came down here to see your mother," Edna remarked, in what seemed to be a non sequitur. But I knew damned well what she was up to.

"You are aware that she spent two weeks with me in New York just a couple of years ago," I said in an attempt to parry her.

"That simply is not the same," she replied. "I know, Archie, that she would love to have you stay with her for a time. It would mean so much to her."

"You say that her health's been good?"

"Well, we are all getting older, you know, that is just a fact of life. Nobody knows just how much time they have left," she said, sidestepping my question.

"Has she been sick in the last few months? She hasn't mentioned anything in her letters, or in the telephone call we had a few weeks ago."

"If there are any problems, she wouldn't talk about it, Archie. And she probably wouldn't say anything to me. You know how she is, never been one to complain."

I was getting frustrated with my aunt's evasiveness, and I saw no benefit in prolonging the conversation, so I told her that I would consider a trip to Ohio at some point, if only to get her off the subject. When Edna pressed me further, I had to bring out the artillery. "I'm sorry, but Mr. Wolfe is signaling me. It seems we have a crisis in a case we're struggling with. I really have to go. It was good talking to you, as it always is."

I hung up and took a deep breath, thinking about my mother. There was no way Edna Wainwright could know that Nero Wolfe never came down to the office from his morning visit with his ten thousand orchids in the greenhouse on the roof until eleven o'clock, which was still more than an hour away.

When Wolfe did come down, by elevator as usual, he carried a raceme of purple Cymbidium, placed it in a vase on his blotter, settled his seventh of a ton into his reinforced chair, and asked if I had slept well. I replied in the affirmative. He then pressed the button in the leg-hole of his desk, which triggered a buzzer in the kitchen that alerted Fritz to bring him two bottles of Remmers beer along with a chilled glass.

As he flipped through the mail I had opened and stacked on his desk, he looked up at me. "Is something troubling you?" he asked.

"No, should it?"

"Your forehead is creased, which is a rare occurrence and one usually brought on by some degree of angst. And yet we have no cases at present for you to stew over," he said, returning to his perusal of the mail.

I long ago gave up trying to mask my feelings from Wolfe, whose radar is always in operation. I reported the telephone conversation with Aunt Edna as he popped the cap off a bottle of beer and poured its contents into the glass, eyeing the foam as it settled. "You of course have not heard the last of that woman, who assuredly will continue to badger you."

"In all probability," I conceded.

"As I just said, we have no case at present, and as you reported to me yesterday, our bank balance is healthier than it has been in months, maybe even in years."

"I take it you're suggesting I go down to Ohio and stick my nose into the death of an old banker?"

"I suggest nothing," Wolfe replied as he picked up his current book, Hitler: A Study in Tyranny, by Alan Bullock. "But such a trip would at least give you an opportunity to visit your mother, with whom you have remained close."

"Who would open your mail and pay the bills and make sure that the orchid germination records are kept up to date?"

"Saul Panzer has on occasion performed those roles and others admirably over the years in your absence—that is, if you have no objection to his sitting at your desk."

"No objection whatever," I said. "That is not to say I am going to Ohio, however." Wolfe chose to make no response, immersing himself in the book.

CHAPTER 2

For the next several days, I gave no thought either to Aunt Edna or to the late Logan Mulgrew, although I was concerned about my mother and considered calling her. Then on a rainy Wednesday morning in the office, I sorted through the bundle that had been delivered by the postal carrier and was surprised to see an envelope bearing my name in neat, precise Palmer Method handwriting.

I rarely receive mail, other than cards from my mother and various siblings on my birthday in October. This letter, in a peach-colored envelope, had a return address that reminded me of what Wolfe had said about Aunt Edna continuing to badger me. Yes, this piece of mail was from her.

I slit the envelope and pulled out its contents, which consisted of a neatly folded letter in a color that matched the envelope, along with a newspaper clipping. First the letter:

Dear Archie,

It was so nice to hear your voice over the wire last week. You sound just as I remember you from years ago. You simply do not seem to age! After our conversation, I felt that you would surely want to see this article, which ran in our local newspaper, the Trumpet, this week. I talked to your mother yesterday, and she seems to be bearing up well, despite the challenges of age that beset us all.

Your loving Aunt Edna

I unfolded the newspaper piece, a column titled Around and About by a writer named Verna Kay Padgett.

QUESTIONS ABOUT BANKER'S DEATH

The recent apparent suicide of longtime bank president Logan Mulgrew has some local residents wondering why a man in such apparent good health would choose to do away with himself. "It makes no sense whatever," said one woman who asked not to be identified. "There is more to this than we are being told. Others agree with me, and I can give you names."

Police Chief Tom Blankenship bristled when I suggested that he look further into Mulgrew's death. "Look, the whole business is cut and dried," he said. "A coroner's jury came up with a verdict of 'death by suicide,' pointing out that he shot himself with a revolver he had a license for.

Period, end of a sad story."

When this reporter pointed out that coroner's juries are nothing more than rubber stamps and do little or no investigating, Chief Blankenship suggested I was guilty of "trying to sensationalize a tragedy," which is not true. I promise my readers that I will continue looking into this case.

Nero Wolfe was right when he said I had not heard the last from Aunt Edna. Her fingerprints were all over that column by Verna Kay Padgett, who probably had been hungering for a big story in a small town for years. She no doubt was an easy prey for Edna's theory.

When Wolfe came down from the plant rooms, I showed him the column, which drew a scowl. "I know and respect your mother, a sensible and intelligent woman who has been a welcome guest here on several occasions. Is her sister so much different that she would indulge herself in what may be a fool's errand?"

"Well, for starters, Edna has always been something of a gossip, no question of that whatever, and if pressed, she would be the first to admit it. I have never known her to subscribe to conspiracy theories, though, which this would seem to be."

Wolfe made a face again. "Do you feel this situation necessitates your presence in that part of the country whence you came?"

"Probably not," I told him, "although this business has gotten me to think more about visiting my mother. As you know, I harbor no nostalgia for what you refer to as 'that part of the country whence I came.' However, it has been several years since I went down there."

"But in the interim, your mother has been to New York numerous times, and she invariably seems to enjoy herself. You go with her to restaurants and plays, and Miss Rowan has taken her to museums and, as I recall, also on what the two women refer to as 'shopping sprees.'"

I grinned. "She and Lily get along very well, no question about that. Maybe you are right. It's probably time I got her to come up here again. I know I would not have to twist her arm, and—" I was interrupted by the ringing of the telephone, which I answered in the usual way during business hours: "Nero Wolfe's office, Archie Goodwin speaking."

It was Aunt Edna, and she sounded breathless. "Archie, you may have thought earlier that I was making a mountain out of a molehill, but you just listen to what has happened: Verna Kay Padgett lives in an apartment on the second floor over Earl Mason's hardware store on Main Street. You remember the shop, it's been there forever. And the night before last, that would be Saturday, someone fired a shot through the window of her living room, where she sometimes writes her columns."

"Was Verna hit?"

"No, fortunately. She said she was in the kitchen at the time. She heard glass breaking, and I know the police have been over at her place investigating."

"It could have been somebody who had a snoot full at some local tavern and then started shooting things up in town on a Saturday night," I said.

"Really, Archie!" my aunt admonished. "I do not know about you, but I do not believe in coincidences, never have. In the first place, I can't remember the last time a firearm was discharged right in the middle of our peaceful town. And in the second place, doesn't it seem strange to you that a bullet was fired through the window in the home of a woman who in print has publicly questioned the cause of the death of one of our leading citizens?"

She had me there. "What is the police chief saying about it?"

"I haven't yet heard. But Mabel Ellis, who knows Verna Kay from hearing her speak at the women's club, says the columnist thinks somebody is out to get her. And I happen to agree. Archie, I really think you need to come down here and put your detective skills to work."

"Aunt Edna, right now is not a good time, for several reasons. But I do understand your concern. I can't talk right now, but I will get back to you." After I hung up, Wolfe looked at me, eyebrows raised.

"You heard enough of that conversation to know that all is not well down Ohio way."

"I did," Wolfe said. "I believe it would put your mind at ease if you paid a visit to your mother—and to your aunt, of course. And I realize you are concerned about your mother's health."

"Are you trying to get rid of me?"

Wolfe drew in a bushel of air and exhaled. "Archie, I believe it would be beneficial for you to visit Ohio. I suspect your mind is down there already. The death of Mr. Mulgrew may prove to be precisely what the local police believe it to be—a suicide. But you have an itch, and you need to scratch it."

"Are you suggesting that I'm curious about Mulgrew's death?"

"I am. I have known you long enough to recognize the signs."

"Which are, other than a creased forehead?"

Wolfe's cheeks deepened into folds, which for him constitutes a smile. "We must have some secrets from each other for life to remain bearable in this house. I am sure I possess traits that betray my feelings and state of mind to you. We are not automatons."

"Which I gather is a fancy word for robots. All right, I will call my mother and tell her to get one of her spare bedrooms ready for the return of the prodigal son."

CHAPTER 3

My mother was at least mildly startled by my suggestion that I pay her a visit. "My heavens, of course I would be delighted to see you," she said. "I am afraid, though, that you are going to find things just as dull around here as you remember them."

"I will take that chance," I said with a chuckle.

"Although," she added, "I should tell you there has been a death in town that some people think is suspicious. Do you remember Logan Mulgrew?"

"The banker."

"The very same. He was found dead at home last week, sprawled on a sofa in his parlor with a hole in his forehead and a pistol next to him."

"Suicide?" I asked, playing the innocent.

"Possibly, although some people, including a local newspaper columnist, seem to think otherwise." My mother did not mention Edna, which probably means my aunt had not shared her suspicions with her sister.

"What is your opinion?" I asked her.

"Well, I certainly would not have thought that Logan Mulgrew was a candidate for suicide. But enough of that. When do you think you will be coming down?"

I told her I planned to leave the next day and would telephone her when I reached Columbus so she could be ready for me. I then wrote checks for all the outstanding bills, got caught up on Wolfe's correspondence, and entered into a file the germination records that orchid gardener Theodore Horstmann had brought down from the plant rooms.

Next, I telephoned my good friend Lily Rowan to tell her about my plans. Calling Lily a "good friend" does not come anywhere close to describing our relationship. We met years ago in an Upstate New York meadow, where I was being chased by an angry bull while involved in a case.* To avoid said animal's horns, I leaped over a fence and sprawled on the ground at the feet of two young women, one of them clad in a yellow shirt and slacks who said to me, "Beautiful! I wouldn't have missed that for anything."

That fetching female in the yellow shirt and slacks, and with blond hair and dark blue eyes, was Lily Rowan, whose companionship I have enjoyed ever since that fateful day. Lily, who still calls me "Escamillo" after the toreador in the opera *Carmen*, is a very wealthy woman, having inherited a fortune from her late father, an Irish immigrant who made his millions by building much of the New York City sewer system.

Lily has a Midtown duplex penthouse apartment where she throws lavish parties, although many of them are fund-raising

---

* *Some Buried Caesar* by Rex Stout

affairs for the various charities she supports. She and I go out on the town frequently, to dinner, dancing, hockey games at Madison Square Garden, and, on occasion, the opera. But just so you know, I always foot the bill.

"So you're off to the place of your origins," Lily said. "I hope your mother is well."

"I hope she is, too, and I will be sure to give her your best."

"Please do, Escamillo, and try to get her back up here to New York. You know how fond I am of her, and how much fun we have hitting the stores along Fifth Avenue."

"I remember all too well the piles of packages you both bring back on your return from those money pits. My plan is to have her stay in the brownstone this fall. You will be the first to know—after Nero Wolfe, of course."

"Of course. Try not to get into any trouble in Ohio."

"Heaven forbid, my dear. See you soon."

That night after a dinner of Fritz's superb curried beef roll with a celery and cantaloupe salad and blueberry pie, Wolfe and I sat in the office with coffee. "I will be leaving for Ohio right after breakfast," I told him. "Everything in the office is up to date, and I have left a note on my desk for Saul Panzer, assuming you'll have need of him."

"I may," Wolfe said. "Have you packed?"

"I've still got a few things to shove into a suitcase, but otherwise, I'm all set. I will take the convertible, of course. That way, Saul can chauffeur you in the Heron if by the rarest of chances you need to leave the brownstone."

"Not likely," Wolfe said, leaning back. "How many miles will you be traveling tomorrow?"

"Several hundred," I told him. Wolfe shuddered. He has a distaste for all motorized vehicles, and he ventures forth as a passenger in an automobile only to visit the barber, or to see the annual Metropolitan Show, or to travel out to Louis Hewitt's Long Island home for his annual dinner there with his fellow orchid fancier. He will only ride in a car if it is driven by me or by Saul Panzer, and even then, he sits tensed in the back seat gripping the passenger strap that had been specially installed.

I said my good-byes to him and went upstairs to finish packing, which included my Marley .32 revolver, just in case. I asked myself what the real reason was for going to Ohio. Was it because the old banker's death intrigued me, or was it concern for my mother? Or was it a combination of the two? I gave up trying to figure it out.

The next morning was as beautiful as anything one could ask for, and it put me in mind of one of the few poetic lines I could remember from my long-ago high school time: "And what is so rare as a day in June?" Just don't ask me who wrote it. I went to get the convertible from Curran's Motors on Tenth Avenue, where we have garaged our cars for years.

"Hey, Archie, you off on another case?" asked Art, a long-time Curran's employee, as he eyed my suitcase.

"It's way too early to say," I told him. "But we have all got to earn a living."

"Yeah, I guess that's true," he said, scratching his head. "But somehow, your way of earning a living seems like it's one hell of a lot more interesting than mine."

"Don't be too sure of that," I replied as we folded down the convertible top. "Some of our work can be pretty dull, like going through court records and running down tips that end up being worthless."

"Hell, I'd still trade places with you," Art said as I climbed behind the wheel and drove away. Traffic in Manhattan was blessedly light that morning as I drove south and entered the

Holland Tunnel that burrowed under the North River, as old-time New Yorkers still refer to the Hudson. I emerged into daylight on the Jersey side, navigating the car through Jersey City, Newark, and a series of suburban towns before finally getting into open country and pressing down on the accelerator.

I had forgotten how small New Jersey is, so the Delaware River came along sooner than I expected. At Trenton I crossed into Pennsylvania, skirting the north edge of Philadelphia and sliding onto the turnpike, which tunneled beneath several tree-covered mountains as I made my way west.

About halfway across the state, I left the pike and stopped for a ham sandwich, a slice of apple pie, and a glass of milk in a white frame diner I encountered along a wooded and twisting country road. The grub might not be up to Fritz's standards, but it was more than bearable, and the well-nourished waitress, whose name tag read *Fran*, was pleasantly chatty.

"I haven't seen you around here before," she said as she wiped the counter with a rag. "How did you happen to stop in?"

"Just luck," I told her. "I was going west on the turnpike and decided to pull off and explore the pleasant countryside."

"Aw, shucks," she said, snapping her fingers. "And here I figured somebody must have told you how good our food is."

"I am not complaining at all. Maybe it was fate that led me here. You seem to be a happy individual."

"My friends call me 'smiley' because it seems that I always look like I don't have a care in the world, which is mainly the case. Compared to others that I know, I have a pretty doggone good life."

I nodded. "I will second that. If I start complaining, I stop and scold myself. I have got little or nothing to gripe about."

"Glad to hear it. Where are you headed, or is that none of my business?"

"To see my mother, two states away. Haven't been back in a while."

"I am sure she will be glad to see you," Fran beamed as I rose to pay the cashier, but not before I had laid a healthy tip on the counter.

I had no intention of getting back on the turnpike and instead headed southwest on winding two-lane roads through Pennsylvania farming country. It was good to have the top down and feel the sun and the warm breeze. I clipped off a corner of West Virginia and crossed the Ohio River into my home state.

This now became a trip backward in time for me as the terrain got hillier and I began to see landmarks that rolled away the years: the well-kept red barn west of Steubenville with the farmer's name printed on it in foot-high white letters; the lake just south of the road with a pier for swimming that had been there since I was a kid; the small-town brick church whose steeple clock had stopped at 5:15 years ago; and the antique store whose weather-beaten sign still proclaimed, "If we haven't got what you're looking for, we will do our darnedest to find it!"

On the outskirts of Columbus, I stopped to get gas, and I used the filling station's pay phone to call my mother.

"This is just about when I expected to hear from you, Archie," she said. "I am beginning to start dinner, and it is one of your favorites."

I knew within minutes how long it would take me to reach my destination, and so did my mother. I started on the last leg of the trip, seeing more familiar sights. After my father died several years ago, Mom sold the farm acreage to a neighbor but kept ownership of the farmhouse. My brother and both my sisters had moved out of state like me, and my mother thought they, and her grandchildren, should have a place to come back to on holidays. And it certainly was a spacious house, with five bedrooms upstairs.

Mom lived alone but was not lonely. The local Presbyterian church occupied a lot of her time. She was chair of the hospitality committee and also filled in when the regular organist was away or indisposed. She regularly visited ailing members of her congregation, played bridge twice a week, and was part of a quilting group. Her own quilts had won awards at the county fair more than once. Mrs. James Arner Goodwin, as she still signed her checks and any legal documents, lived an active life. For the record, she does have a given name—Marjorie.

I arrived in the late afternoon and pulled the convertible into the driveway and parked behind the two-story white frame colonial-style house with its blue shutters on the south edge of town. I hadn't been there in at least seven years, but it appeared as if nothing had changed.

Before I could ring the bell, Mom swung the door open, smiled, and pulled me to her with a hug. "Archie, it is so good to see you. And I am happy to say that you look well fed, although I should not be surprised, given Fritz Brenner's culinary skills."

"You do pretty well in the kitchen yourself," I said, stepping into the cozy living room, where everything seemed to be just the same as I remembered it. "Speaking of kitchens, I detect a very pleasant aroma coming from that direction."

"It's something that I just happen to know you like," she responded. "But you probably want to freshen up before dinner. The north bedroom is all ready for you. Take your time."

I went up to a room I remembered well, with its solid maple bed and matching chest of drawers, the yellow-and-white-striped wallpaper, the painting of the Rocky Mountains at sunrise, and the view down onto Portsmouth Road from a window that was framed by plaid curtains.

When I descended the stairs, Mom was waiting for me at the dining room doorway, arms folded over her chest and a mischievous gleam in her blue eyes. "Dinner is served," she said, gesturing me to the chair at the head of the table.

We sat and she said a brief grace, then took the top off a serving bowl, releasing that aroma I had detected earlier. "Pork tenderloin in casserole, with carrots, celery, and onions," she announced triumphantly. "And a wine I believe you will approve of."

The wine was good, but the pork tenderloin . . . magnificent. "I didn't know you were so good with—"

"So good with this dish, which I happen to know that you particularly like? I was taught by a master, Fritz Brenner by name."

"When did—oh, wait a minute—that time a little over a year ago when you were in New York, one night we had this entrée, didn't we?"

"We did. I asked Fritz about it later, while you and Mr. Wolfe were in the office with coffee. Fritz whispered to me it was one of your favorites and, bless him, he gave me the recipe along with some special instructions."

"Well, this is every bit as good as Mr. Brenner's culinary work," I told her after I had polished off two helpings. "What about this wonderful apple pie?"

"My *own* creation, as you of all people should remember."

"Oh, I do. And don't forget just who picked all those apples from the orchard out back for those pies."

"How well I remember, Archie, although that orchard is long gone. I want you to know how happy I am to have you here, but I also want you to know that I am not a big believer in coincidences."

"Meaning?"

"Meaning I believe that my dear sister has had something to do with your arrival in this usually placid corner of the world."

I paused, trying to pick my words. "Well, I . . ."

"I am not trying to put you on the spot, dear, but for the last several days, Edna has been talking about how she is positive that Logan Mulgrew was murdered. And interspersed with her suspicions have been questions about how you are and how long it has been since you visited here."

I laughed. "I could try to tap-dance around, but you know me too well. It's true that Aunt Edna has been calling and writing me and trying to get me interested in the Mulgrew death."

"It seems to have worked," she said, arching an eyebrow and smiling slyly.

"Maybe, but I don't think I would have driven all the way down here without the added incentive of spending time with you. And one thing you should be aware of: Aunt Edna does not even know yet that I'm here. And just in case she has eyes everywhere in this town, which I suspect, I intentionally parked the car behind the house where it can't be seen from the road."

Now it was my mother's turn to laugh. "Ever the detective. Well, come tomorrow, you probably will want to telephone Edna. You can't stay hidden here forever."

"Good point. Now I would like to spend some time, one, finding out how other members of the family are, and two, getting your thoughts on the life and death of one Logan Mulgrew."

CHAPTER 4

We talked for hours, polishing off the very good wine in the process. At my urging, Mom filled me in on my widely scattered siblings and their children. As to her own health, she professed to be in remarkable shape for her age, although, as she conceded, "Dr. Jensen continues to insist that I need to lose a few pounds, and I continue to insist that I am exactly where I want to be.

"And what about you, Archie?" she asked. "How is your own health? You seem as though you never age, a trait you probably got from your father, who always looked younger than his years. And before I forget, how is our dear Lily?"

"Never better. In fact, just yesterday she asked if you were coming up our way soon. 'I just love it when she's here,' Lily said, 'because it gives me an excuse to shop, shop, shop.' Or words to that effect."

"Not that she needs an excuse," my mother remarked.

"Mr. Wolfe also asked about you and when you might be coming to New York."

"I am surprised to hear that, what with his feelings about women in the brownstone."

"He makes an exception for you—and for Lily, as well. You should really come north in the fall."

"I will, as long as you can assure me that I never get in the way or wear out my welcome."

I gave her that assurance and then switched the topic to Logan Mulgrew. "What do you think happened to him?"

"I don't feel as strongly as my sister seems to that he was killed, but I am not about to rule it out, despite what our young police chief says."

"What was your opinion of Mulgrew?"

"I can't say that I knew him all that well, or his late wife, Sylvia, for that matter. But, overall, I found him to be a rather cold individual, or maybe aloof is a better description. I know how fussy Mr. Wolfe is about usage, so I probably need to choose my words carefully."

"Not around me you don't. Did you do your banking with Mr. Mulgrew?"

"Yes, for years, although neither your father nor I ever dealt with him directly. Only on rare occasions did anyone ever see him in the main banking room downtown. He was usually cloistered behind closed doors wherever the executive suite was, probably upstairs."

"How would you describe his reputation?"

"It depends upon whom you ask. I would say that around our church, he was seen as somewhat godless, probably because he did not belong to any denomination that we were aware of. But that may be an unfair characterization. In my bridge club, the opinions of him were varied, ranging from 'a pillar of the community' to 'a mean, greedy banker.'"

"'That latter description would make him seem like the nasty, small-town banker Lionel Barrymore played in the movie *It's a Wonderful Life*. If Mulgrew was like that, it could have earned him some enemies. Anybody come to mind?"

My mother thought about the question for several seconds, then nodded. "You probably have never heard of Charles Purcell, Archie. About eight years ago, he started the new Merchants Bank to compete with Mulgrew's Farmer's State Bank."

"No, Purcell's name means nothing to me."

"Well, the poor man's endeavor did not last very long at all. It was widely rumored—and Edna would know far more about this than me—that Logan Mulgrew spread the word that the new bank was undercapitalized, and that anyone who put money in it was in danger of losing every cent."

"What about you?"

"I made a modest deposit, just to help Purcell get started. I happen to think competition is healthy, an opinion that I got from your father. But after Mulgrew pulled his scare tactics, there weren't enough of us willing to use his bank, and he finally closed up shop. The word is that all his depositors got their money back. I'm happy to say that I did."

"Mr. Purcell can't have been happy with Logan Mulgrew."

"Not one bit," my mother said. "Again, your aunt Edna probably can tell you more about that, but my understanding is that he, Charles, was rather public in his anger toward Mulgrew."

"Where is Purcell now?"

"That's a sad story, Archie. Because of his own financial losses on the bank failure, they had to sell their house. Charles started drinking heavily, and his wife divorced him and moved in with a sister down in Portsmouth. He now lives with a son and daughter-in-law in town and works as a mechanic in one of our local auto garages. He was always handy with cars, so at least he had that skill to fall back on."

"Would you say the guy was capable of murder?"

Mom set down her now empty wineglass and looked sky-ward, as if seeking heavenly guidance. After a long pause, she said, "I really can't conceive of Charles Purcell killing anyone, but as Edna has said to me more than once, 'You always look for the best in everyone, which often blinds you to their flaws.'"

"You and your sister don't always see eye to eye, do you?"

That brought a smile and a nod. "We love each other, there is no question whatever of that, but there is also a good rea-son that we two old widows don't live together. I'm sure that we would be at each other all the time. I am by nature an optimist, what Edna would call a 'Pollyanna,' while she tends to look for—and find—the faults in everyone, including, I'm sad to say, her own children."

"Ah, the joy of families. Can you think of anyone else who might like to see Mulgrew dead?"

"I was expecting that question, and I have an answer. Do you remember Harold Mapes?"

"The name doesn't sound familiar."

"He had a dairy farm three miles south of here on this very road. It was never as successful as ours, and it seemed like Har-old was always struggling. He got a loan from Mulgrew's bank and then couldn't make the payments. He ended up losing the farm, and he and his wife now work as the tenants on another farm not far away and also on this road, a big spread owned by a man from Columbus. A sad life for a couple in their sixties."

"No doubt he, too, was bitter toward Mulgrew," I said.

"Without question. As is the case with Charles Purcell, Harold has been quite vocal in sharing his feelings toward Mr. Mulgrew. And yet again, I sound like a broken record; Edna could probably tell you more about that. She belongs to our local women's club, and they are much more attuned to what's going on in town than my church circle and bridge club."

"Do you have any other thoughts about possible enemies of Logan Mulgrew?"

"No, I don't, Archie, but you know exactly who to talk to."

"Speaking of Aunt Edna, which we seem to be doing a lot tonight, she mailed me a newspaper column by Verna Kay Padgett that seems to raise questions about Mulgrew's death."

"I read it, too, of course, and I have no doubt that our Edna has the ear of the columnist and reporter."

"She also called to let me know that a bullet was fired through the woman's apartment window."

"Seems that Edna's doing a good job of keeping you up to date on happenings here," my mother said. "Yes, Archie, that shot through the window is what troubles me the most about this whole affair. As you should remember, things here aren't like they are in New York, where I'm sure the sounds of gunfire are common occurrences. It was quite a shock when this happened, although I cannot for the life of me imagine who might have intentionally been shooting at Verna Kay."

"It's not really as bad in New York as you make it out to be, Mom. How do you feel about your police chief?"

"Tom Blankenship? He is a young man, at least by my standards, who grew up here and who worked his way up on the force to become our chief about three years ago. He seems personable and generally well liked, although I have only met him once, at a luncheon in our church fellowship hall. When he became the chief, he made it a point to meet people in churches and at clubs to introduce himself and to ask if anyone had specific concerns."

"Sounds like a smart move. Has he had to deal with any of what you would call big cases since he's been running the force?"

"Oh, there was a holdup at a small grocery store on the

north end of town last year. The store owner called the police after the robbers had left with the money and drove away, heading north on the main road out of town. But the owner got the license number, and a police car, with Tom riding in it, was able to intercept the getaway sedan. There was an exchange of gunshots, with nobody hit, blessedly, and the robber and his driver got out of the car, hands up. That was headline news."

"I guess it would be, all right," I said. "Any idea what Blankenship thinks about the shot fired into the columnist's apartment?"

"There was an item about it in the paper, of course, and all the chief had to say was something like 'We are investigating.'"

"Now that sounds a lot like a New York police statement," I said, "so maybe some things aren't all that different here than in the big bad city."

My mother laughed. "I suppose you should telephone your aunt tomorrow, before she finds out you are with me and wonders why you snuck into town. News travels fast around here, and sooner or later—probably sooner—someone will see you or your car with its New York plates. You can't hide it forever behind the house."

"Point taken. I'll call her right after breakfast."

CHAPTER 5

It had not taken me long to realize that Aunt Edna's ominous suggestions about my mother's health were unfounded and were a ruse to draw me to Ohio and get me interested in the death of Logan Mulgrew. Mom seemed every bit as healthy and vital as she had been on the last two occasions when I had been with her, both of them in New York. And her interests seemed as wide-ranging as ever. I hoped when—or if—I reached her age, I would fare as well.

Her breakfast that morning held its own against Fritz's productions: an omelet with onion, green pepper, tomatoes, and chives; link sausage; bran muffins; cantaloupe slices; and orange juice. And her coffee measured up as well.

"I suppose the time has come for me to call Aunt Edna," I said, sighing as I finished my second cup of coffee. "What are your plans today?"

"I've got a sanctuary guild meeting at church this morning

and bridge in the afternoon," she replied. "Maybe Edna will have you over for lunch."

"Or perhaps I'll pop for it at one of the town's finest spots. Does she have a favorite place to dine?"

"She isn't terribly fussy, and I'm sure she will be delighted to share a meal with you anywhere in town. I'll be leaving in just a few minutes."

"I assume you still drive."

"I do, although not very often at night anymore. And I still use the same car your father had when he died. I make sure I take it to a local garage for regular servicing."

"Is that the same garage where Charles Purcell works?"

"No, we've been going to Beck's Ford dealership for years, and I see no reason to change."

"If it ain't broke, don't fix it, so to speak."

"So to speak," my mother the former English teacher said, rolling her eyes and getting ready to depart for the church. I then dialed Aunt Edna's number, and she answered after several rings.

"It's Archie," I said.

"My goodness, you sound close enough to be next door," she exclaimed.

"I am—almost. I'm staying with Mom. I just got in last evening." There was a long pause at the other end.

"My goodness—oh, I'm repeating myself, aren't I? Marjorie's, she's . . . all right, isn't she?"

"Absolutely. I thought I might drop by and see you this morning. Mom's gone off to a meeting at church."

"Oh yes, yes, please come by. I live right in town now. Unlike your mother, I didn't stay in the farmhouse after Melvin died. Too many memories, I suppose."

She gave me her address, along with some directions, which I didn't need as the town had not changed all that much. After a ten-minute drive, I pulled up in front of a two-story Cape Cod house a short walk from the town square that looked like it was lifted off a Hollywood suburban set, complete with the freshly painted white picket fence that enclosed a small front yard of well-tended grass as lush as a putting green.

"Dear Archie!" Aunt Edna said as she pulled open the front door while my finger still hovered over the button. "It has been years since I have laid eyes on you, simply years," she added while reaching up to squeeze me. "Your mother gets to see you more than I do because she travels to New York every two or three years."

If she was hoping I would suggest she accompany Mom on her next trip north, she would be disappointed. My mother has made it clear to me that her sister is best taken in relatively small doses.

I stepped into a small entry hall and then a living room that reflected Aunt Edna's love of antiques. This was not a room a man would feel comfortable in, as the chairs and even the sofa looked like they would collapse under the weight of a normal-sized male.

But at my aunt's urging, I sat on the sofa while she went to the kitchen for coffee. When she brought in cups for each of us, she sat opposite me in a chair that looked like it was already old when Paul Revere rode his horse through the Massachusetts countryside to warn his neighbors that the Redcoats were coming.

"Please be honest, Archie," she said after taking a sip of coffee. "Did you come to town to see your mother or because I asked you?"

"A little of each," I told her. "But now that I'm here, I am interested in learning more about your thoughts on Mulgrew's death."

"Let me ask you a question first," my aunt said. "What did your mother say about Logan Mulgrew? I am sure the subject must have come up yesterday or this morning."

"It did. Mom described him as 'cold, aloof, and godless.'"

"All true, Archie—but much more. He was a mean, vindictive individual who didn't care a whit about other people or their feelings."

"Please don't hold back."

That brought a smile from Edna, who really did have a sense of humor. "One more question about your dear mother: Did she have any thoughts about who might have done away with Logan?"

"Before we go any further, I want to take you to lunch after we finish our coffee. Is there a spot nearby that you like?"

"Caldwell's is a pleasant spot, just three blocks from here," she said. "You won't remember it because it doesn't date back to your years living here."

Caldwell's turned out to be a typical small-town café, booths lining one wall, tables in the middle of the room, and a row of stools at the Formica-topped counter. The walls were covered with black-and-white photographs showing scenes of the town in earlier times.

We settled into a booth and ordered, a club sandwich for Edna and chili for me. "Back to my earlier question, Archie," she said. "Did your mother have any thoughts as to who might have killed Logan Mulgrew?"

"When I posed that question to her, she told me about two men, Charles Purcell and Harold Mapes, who did not like the banker."

"That is putting it mildly! They detested him. But they are not the only ones who had reason to dislike Logan."

"Go on, you have my undivided attention."

"Oh, where to start? Did your mother happen to mention Lester Newman?"

I shook my head and Edna continued. "His sister, Sylvia, had been married to Mulgrew for, well, forever, it seems. When she died a little over a year ago, Newman was outraged and made no attempt to hide his anger. Sylvia, who had a heart condition and also had become more than a little senile, died from an overdose of her digitalis heart medication, and her brother, who lives down south of here in Waverly, was absolutely convinced that Mulgrew had fed her that overdose, and that in her mental condition she wouldn't have realized it."

"Just why would he want his wife dead?"

Edna leaned forward, as if about to share a secret. "Aha, I knew, being the good detective you are, that you would ask that question. There was, shall we say, someone else in Logan Mulgrew's life."

"A little old to be chasing around, wasn't he?"

"He may have been old, but he certainly didn't act his age," Aunt Edna huffed. "And this wasn't the only time in recent years that he was frisky. But then, I'm getting ahead of myself. One flirtation at a time."

"Go on, I am all ears," I told her.

"During Sylvia's last months, Logan brought in a young and very attractive woman to be her caregiver."

"Don't tell me that she—"

"You know where I am going, don't you, Archie? This thirty-two-year-old, named Carrie Yeager, settled into the Mulgrew house and also made herself at home with the lord and master, if you get my drift."

"And just how do you know this?"

"It didn't take a genius to figure out what was going on. Carrie and Mulgrew started being seen around town in restaurants on numerous occasions. Oh, they weren't acting lovestruck or anything like that; they both were too smart."

"It seems there's only circumstantial evidence of an affair," I observed.

"Perhaps, but just how often do the caregiver and the spouse of the patient need to consult—and over dinner at that? And there's more: After Sylvia's death, Miss Yeager moved out of the house and took an apartment in that new postwar-style four-story building on the square downtown. And who do you suppose was seen more than once going into that building?"

"I have a feeling that you are going to tell me."

Aunt Edna nodded, lips pursed. "So now you can see why Newman saw Logan Mulgrew for what he was—an out-and-out philanderer. And his own sister was the victim of this, this . . . *dalliance.* As far as I'm concerned, that sort of behavior could cause a man like Newman to do violence, and some people might not blame him."

"Possibly," I said. "Does Miss Yeager still live in that apartment building?"

"Interesting you should ask. She moved out a week or two ago, from what I have been hearing via the grapevine. And nobody I've talked to seems to know where she's gone."

"Not even that newspaper woman of yours, Verna Kay Padgett?"

"Not even Verna Kay, although I wouldn't be surprised to learn that she's done some checking up."

"I definitely want to meet Miss Padgett. Have the police learned anything about that shot that was fired through her window?"

"If they have, I am not aware of it."

"I don't suppose you have any other suspects to run by me."

"Oh yes I do, Archie. A man named Eldon Kiefer, whom I'm sure you have not heard of."

"You're right. What was his beef with Logan Mulgrew?"

"His daughter, Becky, worked as a secretary in Farmer's State Bank, and Mulgrew, so the story goes, took liberties with the young woman, supposedly against her will."

"And let me guess—she then refused to press charges, right?"

"Right. She is a very shy young woman, without a lot of self-confidence. I've heard that her father urged her to speak out, but she refused."

"I hope she didn't keep working for that so-and-so."

"No, and she did not even want to stay in town anymore, which was certainly understandable. She ended up moving to Cleveland, where she has an apartment and a job with another bank, or so it's said. You won't be surprised to hear that Farmer's State gave her a great recommendation."

"Anything to get her out of town, eh?"

"That's right, Archie. But you had better believe that her father remained irate with Logan and would have gone to the police himself if his daughter hadn't begged him not to."

"You seem to have awfully good sources," I said.

"Your mother thinks I'm a gossip, as you probably know. But people just seem to tell me things." *Yeah, and you go out of your way to encourage that*, I thought but held my tongue. No sense alienating a good source. "So is that it as far as suspects that you are aware of?"

"Isn't that enough?" Aunt Edna answered, tilting her chin at me and folding her arms across her chest.

"It hardly makes Logan Mulgrew look like an exemplary member of the community," I conceded. "Just out of curiosity, do you know who Mulgrew left his estate to?"

"I do," my aunt said in a smug tone. "It just so happens that a friend of mine is married to the lawyer who handled Mulgrew's financial matters. Mulgrew and his wife had no children, so all

his financial holdings go to his grandniece, Donna, and the proceeds from the sale of his house are to be given to the Salvation
Army, so at least the man was possessed of some of the milk of
human kindness."

"You have a nice way with words, Aunt Edna. And now I
would like to talk to that columnist, Verna Kay Padgett."

"I would be happy to introduce you."

CHAPTER 6

I thanked my aunt for the offer, but I knew that if she did introduce us, she would insist on hanging around and making any conversation a three-way event. I wanted to hear what the reporter/columnist had to say without her being prompted or getting interrupted, so I suggested to Edna that she telephone Verna Kay Padgett to set up an appointment for the two of us.

Once we were back at Aunt Edna's house after lunch, she called the newspaper. "Verna Kay says that she is intrigued about meeting a real, honest-to-goodness New York detective," Edna said after hanging up. "She has heard of Nero Wolfe and said that anybody who works for him must be good."

"Well, that is a start anyway," I replied. "I'm interested in what else she has to say."

We were to meet at three that afternoon in the offices of the *Trumpet* downtown. As I walked through the business district,

I observed that the town seemed to have changed very little in the years since I had last spent time there. And it was essentially the same if one went even farther back to the dark ages, when my only mode of transportation had been a bicycle. Now as then, the population hovered around twenty thousand, and new construction was minimal, other than the downtown apartment building Aunt Edna had referred to, along with a handful of ranch-style houses in a north side development that went bankrupt almost as soon as it had begun breaking ground.

Only a single movie theater remained of the three I'd haunted as a grade-schooler, but at least the survivor had been the best of the trio, the one that always showed the latest films and had the most-buttery popcorn. Feeble attempts had been made to spruce up many of the buildings along the main drag, but these half-hearted facelifts soon began to prove that a couple of coats of paint and a new sign were no match for brutal midwestern winters and fierce spring thunderstorms.

Still, the small city gamely soldiered on and was able to sustain the loss of its largest employer, a company producing railroad wheels, by luring into the same plant a business that manufactured motorized recreational vehicles, which were becoming popular. The best news of all, according to a letter my mother had sent me at the time, was that the new operation would have as many people on its payroll as the old one.

The *Trumpet* still occupied the two-story brick building where it had been during my growing-up years, when I delivered the paper every weekday on my bike. I walked in and was greeted by a smiling young woman behind a waist-high counter.

"Good afternoon, sir. Are you here to place a classified advertisement?" When I replied that I was to meet with Verna Kay, she pointed to a door on the left. "She will be at the first desk you come to in our newsroom, sir." I felt older each time she called me *sir*.

I was expecting a prim, middle-aged columnist much like Cora Ann Wilson, who had been a guest speaker in one of my high school classes and who had preached to us students the importance of getting as many local residents mentioned in print as possible. "People love to see their names in the paper, and always in a positive context, of course," Cora Ann had said in a tone that brooked no argument.

The first desk I came to was occupied by a slender woman in her twenties with long, chestnut hair, a straight nose that was just the right length, and the heart-shaped face of one who might earlier have been a homecoming queen. "I am looking for Verna Kay Padgett," I said, fully expecting to eventually encounter a carbon copy of Cora Ann Wilson.

"You have found her, and you must be Mr. Goodwin," she replied, standing, smoothing her skirt, and giving me a dimpled smile that lit up the room. "It is so nice to meet you."

I think I recovered from my surprise and took the slender hand that was offered to me. "Your aunt said you wanted to talk about Logan Mulgrew's death," Verna Kay said. "May I suggest we have coffee down at White's Rexall Drugs? I don't have any deadlines right now."

"Fine by me," I told her, "but only with the stipulation that I buy."

She agreed, and we set off for the drugstore. "How long have you been at the *Trumpet*?" I asked as we walked along the shop-lined streets.

"Just over two years now, ever since I graduated from the state university over in Athens with a journalism degree. And very honestly, just between us, I am ready to move on to a larger paper in a larger city. I've sent résumés to dailies in both

Toledo and Cleveland, but I would prefer you keep that to yourself."

"Consider it done. Are things a little too quiet for you here?"

That brought another smile. "Such is the case most of the time, but I had to get my start somewhere. The bigger papers that I applied to before I graduated told me I needed to get some experience first, and the *Trumpet* happened to have an opening."

"And so now you are getting that experience," I said as we entered the drugstore and perched on stools at the marble-topped lunch and soda counter. "Do you believe Logan Mulgrew killed himself?"

"You get right to the point, don't you? I like that, no beating around the bush. I'm sure that's the mark of a good detective. In answer to your question, I think his death was very suspicious. I interviewed him once, and he seemed to be healthy and in fine shape for his age. Why should he want to kill himself?" Verna Kay posed as we were served coffee.

"My aunt has asked the same question."

"Your aunt is quite a character, isn't she? And I mean that in a positive way. I assume she has shared her theories with you."

"That she has. What do you think of those theories of hers?"

"There is no question whatever that Logan Mulgrew had made more than his share of enemies over the years. You don't have to spend much time in this town to learn that. I come from a town way over near Cincinnati, but within a few weeks of moving here, I began to hear stories about him, and many of them were not very nice stories."

"By chance, did you happen to get some of these stories from my aunt?"

The color rose in Verna Kay's cheeks. "Well . . . she certainly has been a good source of local lore. But just so you know, Mr.

Goodwin, everything I have heard from Edna I also verified through other sources."

"That sounds like a good reporting procedure, and before we go any further, please call me Archie."

"I will, and I go by Katie to my friends, who gave me that name in college. I've never liked being called Verna, but I was named for my favorite aunt, so what can you do but live with it until you're old enough to choose an alternative?"

"It seems to me that Katie is a fine alternative. Now . . . tell me what you have concluded, if anything, about the demise of one Logan Mulgrew."

"I am sure that he was killed, Archie," she said in what I would term an intense whisper, if there is such a thing.

"A few minutes ago, you called Mulgrew's death 'extremely suspicious.' Now, all of a sudden, you seem to have a more definite opinion."

"I'm guessing your aunt told you about a shot that was fired through my apartment window."

"I was going to get to that, but since you brought the subject up, tell me what you think about it."

"Gunfire is very rare around here, making it very unlike conditions in New York."

"Now you sound like my mother, who thinks the big city is an armed camp. This despite the fact that she's been to visit me in New York several times and has yet to hear a single gunshot."

"I'm sorry, Archie," Katie said, shaking her head. "I know that I can be guilty of stereotyping. My point was that because gunfire is so rare around here, I don't believe that shot to be a coincidence."

"I shouldn't think you would. What do the local police say about what happened—especially Blankenship?"

"Have you met him?"

"No, remember that I just got here yesterday. I've heard a little about him from my mother and my aunt. Give me your take on the man."

She shrugged. "He's all right, I suppose, and certainly earnest enough. But I'm not sure he's got enough experience to deal with what sure looks like a murder. He's behaving, at least publicly, like he still believes Mulgrew's death was a suicide."

"How does he explain the shot through your window?"

"He said he thinks it was just some guy who became trigger-happy after getting loaded in some bar. After all, he stressed that this did occur on a Saturday night, when, as he pointed out, some locals do get tanked up."

"Even though gunshots, as you pointed out, are very rarely heard in these parts."

"Unless you count hunters," Katie Padgett said, "and this isn't hunting season."

"Was the incident covered by the *Trumpet*?"

"Yes, but not by me; another reporter on the staff wrote about it. They wouldn't have wanted me to write about something in which I was the subject. That is simply not a good journalism practice."

"Understood. Was Blankenship quoted in the article?"

Katie nodded. "He said pretty much what I just mentioned, about somebody getting drunk and going on a Saturday night toot."

"Did anyplace else in town get shot up that night?"

"You ask very good questions, Archie. You would have made a fine reporter if you hadn't decided to be a detective."

"Aw shucks, it's just my inborn curiosity. I repeat my query."

"Of course, I posed that to Tom Blankenship, and he said no other gunshots were reported in town that night."

"When's the last time you talked to Blankenship, either on the telephone or in person?"

"That was the last time. He hasn't returned any of my calls since then. I really don't believe he wants to speak to me."

"Do you think the chief is honest and efficient?"

"I do, but I also believe that he is in over his head on the Mulgrew death."

"So it's safe to say he hasn't interviewed anyone about what happened, right?"

"That's true, with the exception of a grandniece, Donna Newman, the granddaughter of Mulgrew's brother-in-law. She's the one who found her uncle dead in his living room with a bullet wound to the head and a pistol on the sofa cushion beside him. She went to the house when he hadn't been at the bank for two days and his telephone at home went unanswered."

"Didn't the man have some sort of live-in or part-time help?"

"You would think with his money that he would have," Katie answered, "but he is said to have prided himself on his independence. He cooked his own meals when he wasn't eating out, and he did his own housecleaning, according to his grandniece. I suspect that he was a skinflint."

"Have you talked to the niece?"

"I have, and she seems to be genuinely broken up about her great-uncle's death. Donna, who is single and is a high school English teacher in a town about thirty miles west of here, told me she made it a point to stop by and see him once or twice every week. She naively seemed to overlook the faults that others saw in the man."

"And the niece felt that he had killed himself?"

"She told me that she wasn't really sure. On the one hand, she said her great-uncle had been somewhat despondent because of his wife's death, but on the other hand, she said that in the days before he died, he seemed to have a renewed interest in life, although she wasn't quite sure what had caused it. She seemed to be of two minds on how he died."

"Now Verna Kay, or rather, Katie, I would like to get your thoughts on who you think might have wanted Logan Mulgrew dead."

CHAPTER 7

Katie, as I now refer to Verna Kay Padgett, coughed nervously and drained the coffee from her cup. "Okay, now if I am repeating things that your aunt already has told you, let me know."

"Let us not worry about dear Aunt Edna. It is your perspective that I'm interested in."

"Okay, here we go," she said, coughing again, apparently a nervous habit. "A local man named Charles Purcell started a bank here several years ago, and Mulgrew did not like the new competition one bit. He had been used to having things all his own way for years, so he methodically went about sabotaging the Purcell operation by starting rumors that it was undercapitalized, and that depositors were likely to lose every cent they deposited."

"Was there any evidence this was true?"

"Not that I have been able to learn. Bear in mind that much of this happened well before I arrived in town, but I have talked to at least a dozen residents, and several of them felt Mulgrew was just plain fighting dirty."

"Did any of the people you talked to make deposits in the new Purcell bank?"

Katie smiled. "Good question. A few did, but several others admitted they were scared away and later regretted it, or so they then claimed."

"Talk is cheap. Where were those folks when the man needed them to get his operation going? And where is Purcell now?" I asked, knowing the answer but wanting to get Katie's perspective.

"His bank's failure wiped out the man financially, and he ended up having to sell his house to pay his debts. He started drinking heavily, his wife left him, and he now lives in town with his son and daughter-in-law. He was always good with cars, so now he works as a mechanic for a local garage."

"Well, at least the man's employed," I said.

"Yes, that's the good news, such as it is," Katie said. "The bad news is that, as I said, he has hit the bottle pretty hard, and he's been heard in a bar just down the street from here cursing out Mulgrew and using threatening words like 'that vicious son of a bitch.'"

"Sounds like a potential murder suspect, all right. Who else is a possibility?"

"A dairy farmer named Harold Mapes, who borrowed money from Mulgrew's bank. Then he had a bad year—some sort of cow disease is what I heard—and he didn't have the money to keep up his interest payments. Mulgrew foreclosed on him, and he lost the farm. He and his wife now work as tenants on another farm nearby, owned by a man from out of town, I think. Mapes is bitter, as you would suspect, and like Purcell, he has been heard to berate Mulgrew, saying things like 'I'd like to strangle that son of a gun.' Except he didn't use 'son of a gun.'"

"It seems that Logan Mulgrew could win the 'Town's Most Hated' award."

"I'm not done, Archie, there's a lot more. Your aunt may have mentioned Lester Newman, who was a brother-in-law of Mulgrew and also the grandfather of Donna, the one who found Mulgrew dead." I nodded but said nothing, Katie's cue to continue.

"Newman, who people I've talked to say is mentally unstable, is absolutely convinced that Logan Mulgrew killed his wife, Sylvia, by giving her an overdose of her heart medicine."

"Had she lived with a coronary condition for a long time?"

"Several years, and she also had become increasingly senile, hence her death was ruled as accidental, the assumption being that she unwittingly gave herself an overdose."

"Sounds plausible on the surface," I remarked.

"Maybe, but from what I hear, Newman was convinced that Mulgrew killed his wife because he was having an affair with the woman who was brought in to be his wife's caregiver."

"What do you think of that theory?"

"Despite his age, Mulgrew apparently still had, shall we say . . . strong urges," she said, her cheeks coloring. "And he had yielded to these urges on several occasions in the past, if the talk around town can be believed."

"Some things don't change," I said. "I grew up in and around this burg years ago, and it was always filled with what you refer to as 'talk.' I seem to remember there were gossipmongers every-where—with the exception, I am happy to say, of my mother."

"But not the exception of your aunt?" Katie posed with eye-brows raised.

"No, I don't except Aunt Edna. She has always been inter-ested, perhaps *too* interested, in the activities of her neighbors and other townspeople. As I'm sure you have learned, there aren't too many secrets in these smaller towns. Tell me about this caregiver Mulgrew's wife had."

"That would be Carrie Yeager, a professional nurse. I have seen her only once, at that pro forma coroner's inquest into Sylvia Mulgrew's death. She must be in about her midthirties and is quite attractive—tall, slender, dark-haired, and with a figure that attracts second looks, particularly from men. She generated a lot of talk around town."

"And the *talk*—ah, there's that word again—is that Miss Yeager, I assume she's a miss, was involved with the late Mr. Mulgrew."

"Yes, Carrie is single, or possibly divorced. And it was more than talk, of that I am absolutely sure," Katie said. "While she was Sylvia's caregiver, she dined out frequently with Mulgrew, presumably to discuss the bedridden woman's condition. And after Sylvia's death, the two continued to be seen at local restaurants fairly often."

"And she stayed in Mulgrew's house?" I asked.

"Oh no, they were not quite as blatant as all that. After the wife's funeral, Carrie moved into an apartment downtown, and Mulgrew was spotted visiting her there. And they also kept on dining together, at least a few times a week."

"Where is Carrie now?"

"Nobody seems to know. A few days after Mulgrew's death, she moved out of her apartment and hasn't been seen around town. And by the way, she did not go to his funeral."

"I gather you were there. Was it well attended?"

"Sort of," Katie said. "A lot of people from the bank, of course, and a scattering of others, including a few local businessmen who probably showed up because they wanted to stay on good terms with the bank. There were also a few older ladies there, including your aunt."

"I'm sure Edna has never been one to miss a funeral, whether she liked the deceased or not. So our caregiver disappeared without a trace?"

"I don't believe anyone has tried very hard to locate her, Archie. And remember, our police chief would hardly bother, given that he does not suspect foul play, to use a phrase I'm sure you're familiar with."

"Foul play? Sure, I use those words all the time," I said with a wink. "We private eyes would be lost without them in our vocabularies, along with 'dames,' 'gats,' 'thugs,' and 'coppers.' Now, have we covered all the people who might have wanted to see Logan Mulgrew six feet under?"

"I can think of one other person who bears consideration," Katie said as she pivoted on her stool to face me. "His name is Eldon Kiefer, and his daughter, Becky, was once one of Mulgrew's secretaries at the bank."

"Go on."

"You probably have an idea where I'm heading with this, Archie. Kiefer accused Mulgrew of sexually molesting his daughter and getting her pregnant—a pregnancy that is supposed to have ended with an abortion, location unknown. Not surprisingly, Kiefer threatened Mulgrew, who of course denied having any sort or relationship with the girl. He, Mulgrew, acted outraged and claimed that Becky had an overactive imagination. I wanted to write something about all this, but my lily-livered bosses on the paper thought it would open us up to lawsuits."

"What did Becky have to say about what happened?"

"Ah, there lies part of the problem: she apparently does not have a lot of self-confidence, and if what I've heard is true, she begged her father not to press charges against Mulgrew."

"But she did have an abortion?" I posed.

"That has not even been established, and I'm not sure how it could be verified. After all, a lot of these abortion mills are backstreet operations. And Becky sure isn't about to tell us anything—if indeed the abortion really took place. I've tried to call her repeatedly without success."

"Speaking of Becky, what is she doing now?" I asked.

"Working at a bank up in Cleveland, and living there in an apartment, as far as I've been able to tell."

"Does her father live around here?"

"Yes, Kiefer is a long-distance truck driver, who has a house in town with his wife. He is a strange duck, withdrawn and not given to socialization, according to those I've spoken to who know him. Also, he hangs out in a local tavern, not unlike Purcell. The only time I got hold of him on the telephone, he hung up on me after suggesting that I 'go straight to hell.'"

"You mentioned earlier that you interviewed Mulgrew once. What were the circumstances?"

"It was just after I arrived here, and one of my editors thought I should do a piece on him, to get his slant on the community and what he thought its economic health was."

"How did that go?"

"To use his quote, he said that 'things have never been better, it's clear that our little city has a great future, and I'm proud to be part of it.'"

"Quite the booster, including of himself, I gather."

"I'll say. He insisted on being interviewed at home, which . . . well, which made me uncomfortable."

"Even though I'm sure he had a plush office at the bank," I said.

"Of course. But my editors liked the idea of my describing what his house looked like, or at least his living room."

"Nothing like local color, right?"

"Yes. My editors thought the interview needed a woman's touch, including the style of the furniture, et cetera," she replied, rolling her eyes.

"I'm sure nobody at the university ever told you that being a female newspaper reporter was going to be easy."

That got a laugh. "One of my professors, a crusty old guy with a white mustache—at least he seemed old to me—once said, 'Look, Padgett, this may be the 1950s, but girl reporters are still in a minority, and you are going to have to work twice as hard as a man to get the same amount of credit, and probably without the same amount of pay.'"

"Just what you needed in the way of encouragement," I said.

"Unfortunately, he was right, Archie. This is still very much a man's game, but I'm doing what I can to compete. I just wish that at least one of my bosses at the *Trumpet* was a woman."

"Maybe things will change," I told her, not believing it. "What made you uncomfortable when you interviewed Mulgrew?"

She shrugged. "It's hard to put into words, but for one thing, he had me sit on a couch and then he sat down next to me—*right* next to me. And he kept looking me up and down, like he was more interested in me than in answering my questions. He seemed to like my legs. I couldn't wait to get out of there. At least he never put his hands on me."

"Well, that's something anyway. Do you have any other possible suspect to parade before me?"

"Aren't there enough?" she said with a smirk. "As a detective, maybe you now have some thoughts about all this."

"Katie, I am still in the process of digesting everything you and others have told me. Please bear in mind that although I am indeed a detective, and I have a license issued by the sovereign state of New York to prove it, I am by no means Nero Wolfe, not even close, either in girth or in brainpower."

"Well, I am still impressed. Will you promise to sometime tell me about a few of your cases? I would love to hear about them."

"It's a deal," I said as we left the drugstore and parted company at the *Trumpet* offices. I then headed back to the house on the edge of town where I spent what would be termed my formative years.

CHAPTER 8

"Well, how did your visit with my sister go today?" my mother asked when I breezed in the front door.

"She was as talkative as you would expect," I said, "and she was filled with stories about a number of people who had reasons to dislike Logan Mulgrew."

"I can only imagine how animated she was in discussing all those people. Edna must have really been in her element. She would have made a fine gossip columnist. Were you also able to see the *Trumpet* reporter?"

"I was, and I didn't expect her to be so young. Say, I hope you haven't started dinner yet."

"No, I was thinking that tonight we might have—"

"Say no more," I told her, holding up a hand like a Forty-Second Street traffic cop during the evening rush. "I did not come all the way down to this bucolic corner of our fine nation just to have you prepare a meal for me every night, as good as your cooking is. We are going out to dinner, and it's my treat."

"*Bucolic*, you say? Mr. Wolfe has done wonders for your vocabulary."

"Lily has, too, but don't try to change the subject. You must have a favorite restaurant around here."

"In truth, I don't have occasion to eat out all that much," my mother said. "But I do have a place that I have come to like, an Italian restaurant that opened up just a year ago downtown. Edna took me there for my birthday, which is how I got introduced to it. The food is quite good—surely not up to Fritz Brenner's standards—but then, where in the world are you going to find a place that is?"

"I am in the mood for pasta. Let's go!"

Because it was still early, the restaurant wasn't crowded, and we were able to get a booth along the back wall. The owners had fitted the place out to resemble one of those dark and cozy Italian eateries so prevalent in New York and, I'm sure, in other large cities as well.

We ordered from a white-aproned young man whose face had Naples written all over it. He quickly poured us each a glass of Chianti from a bottle encased in a wicker basket and went about describing the daily specials in detail.

"They have done a nice job of evoking a mood," I observed. "Have they been doing a good business?"

"I think so," my mother said. "I have only been here on three occasions, but each time it was crowded, and I'm sure it will be in a few more minutes."

Sure enough, people began drifting in, in pairs and groups, and soon the restaurant was almost full.

"Well, look who just entered, Archie. That tall man with the woman in the gray dress is our police chief, Tom Blankenship."

"I would like to meet him," I said, "and he is going to have to come by us to get to that last open table."

"Hello, Chief Blankenship," my mother said, "I am not sure that you remember me, Marjorie Goodwin."

"Of course, I remember you, Mrs. Goodwin, from that time I spoke at a luncheon in your church," Blankenship said with an ingratiating grin. He had a strong jaw, close-cropped black hair, and dark eyes that seemed to be searching for something. "You were one of the hostesses, as I recall. This is my wife, Eleanor."

"And this is my son, Archie."

"Oh yes," Blankenship said, shaking hands as I stood. "I know you by reputation. Yours was one of the short biographies in the newspaper last year of former residents who have gone on to greater things elsewhere. I had of course heard of Nero Wolfe, and I was interested to learn that you are his right-hand man."

"He is the brains behind the operation," I replied. "I'm just a glorified water carrier."

"I doubt that very much. After all your adventures in New York, you must find life to be very boring in these parts," the chief said.

"I'm rarely bored," I said. "I seem to find things to keep me busy."

"Well, that is good to know," Blankenship replied, unsure of what else to say. "It was nice to meet you; will you be staying here long?"

"It's too early to tell; I may be around awhile." With that, Blankenship and his wife excused themselves and went to their table across the room.

"Before you utter a single word, Archie," my mother said, "I had nothing whatever to do with that thumbnail biography of you that ran in the *Trumpet*. I happen to know it was your aunt's work, because she bragged to me about what she had done. I told her that you would not be at all happy if you ever found out about it."

"Don't worry, when Blankenship mentioned it, I knew exactly who was behind that article. But that's just Aunt Edna being Aunt Edna."

After we had gotten our food—spaghetti for Mom and lasagna for me—she asked, "What did you think of our police chief?"

"Young, and he seems to be earnest. Beyond that, not much to go on, although I have to wonder if he might be suspicious about why I happen to be here."

"Do you think so, Archie? There's nothing so very unusual about a son visiting his mother, even if that son just happens to be a New York private detective."

"Maybe not. I just sensed he was sizing me up."

"Well, after all, you are well known. Now I want to repeat a question I started to ask before we left the house: Did you ever talk to that *Trumpet* reporter?"

"Oh yes, I did, and for quite a while. She has lots of thoughts about people who had reasons to dislike Mulgrew. Do you know Verna Kay?"

"Not well. Oh, I have met her a few times, including once at our church, where she talked at a luncheon, just like Blankenship did. We try to get local speakers in to tell us about their work. She struck me as being quite ambitious and self-confident."

"I think at least some of that self-confidence may have been shaken by the bullet that got fired into her apartment."

"Yes, that is certainly troubling, Archie. At the risk of behaving like Edna, I'm curious as to whom Verna Kay sees as suspects in what I gather she thinks is a murder."

"Katie definitely thinks that Mulgrew was killed. Among others who disliked him, she talked about Purcell and Mapes, both of whom you had mentioned."

"Katie?" my mother asked, eyebrows raised.

"Yes, that is what Verna Kay calls herself now. She doesn't like the name Verna."

"It seems to me that the two of you are getting pretty friendly."

"It's all in a day's work, Mom."

That brought a titter. "All right, what else does *Katie* have to say about those others she mentioned?"

"There are a number of them, all of whom your sister also talked about. One is Lester Newman, the brother of Sylvia Mulgrew, who thinks the banker poisoned Sylvia by giving her an overdose of her heart medication. Newman seems to believe Mulgrew wanted to get rid of his wife because he was having an affair with her caregiver, a nurse named Carrie Yeager. Had you heard anything about that?"

"Only from Edna," my mother replied with what I would describe as a wry grin. "I don't move in circles where there is a lot of that kind of information exchanged."

"So your sister supplies it to you?"

"Not necessarily by my choice. What else did your Katie have to say?"

"She is by no means *my* Katie, Mom. She told me about a man named Eldon Kiefer, whom Edna also had mentioned. He has a daughter, Becky, who once worked as a secretary in Mulgrew's bank."

"I believe I may have met her once or twice at the bank, although I never knew her last name. An attractive girl, as I recall."

"Apparently Mulgrew thought so, too, because he is supposed to have gotten very personal with young Miss Kiefer, to the point where she may have become pregnant."

"Oh my, I really do not seem to know what's going on all around me," my mother said, bringing a hand to her mouth in mock surprise. "So am I to gather that Edna and our girl reporter both think Kiefer might have killed Logan Mulgrew?"

"That's what *I* gather. Becky has left town and now lives up in Cleveland, where it's said that she works for a bank."

"Was she indeed pregnant?"

"Nobody seems to know that for sure, Mom. She may or may not have gotten an abortion."

My mother shook her head and looked sad. "I don't know Eldon Kiefer. I assume he's married."

"Yes, according to what I have learned, and he's somewhat antisocial, pretty much keeps to himself. He earns his living as a long-distance trucker."

"There was a time, way back when we moved here, that this town felt much smaller than today, although I know the population has been fairly stable," my mother said. "It seemed like your father and I knew almost everyone. That is not the case now, and I am not sure which way is better. We knew more people then, but also everyone seemed to know everyone else's business. Now, life seems to be more anonymous."

"I would cast my vote for the way things are now," I said. "I can remember when I was a kid in school that my classmates were filled with stories about whose father was a drunk or a bad debtor and whose mother was sleeping with the grocer or the plumber. Maybe it's the New Yorker in me talking, but I think there's something to be said for a certain amount of anonymity."

"I guess I agree, Archie, although I hardly think your aunt does."

I laughed. "Oh no, Edna still seems to have her feelers out as to who's doing what to whom and why. Well, enough of dissecting the town. I have to say the food here is first-rate."

"Now you didn't think I would lead you into some greasy spoon, did you, Archie?"

As I finished my lasagna, I reflected on how heartening it was to see that my mother still had verve, animation, and a healthy sense of humor. It was good to be back home . . . at least for a while.

Back at the house and up in "my" bedroom, I took stock: Should I push ahead and investigate Mulgrew's death? I voted yes.

CHAPTER 9

In the morning, I called Katie at the *Trumpet*. "Hi, Archie, it's good to hear your voice. What can I do for you today?"

"I would like to meet Logan Mulgrew's grandniece, Donna. I know she lives and teaches in a town several miles west of here. Do you have her phone number and address?"

"I do, and I would be happy to introduce you. She seems to be a very nice girl."

"Thanks, but that is not necessary. What you could do, however, is give her a call and tell her she will be hearing from me. That would pave the way, and she won't think I'm some sort of creep."

"Are you sure that you don't want me along?"

"Nothing personal, but I usually do my interviewing one-on-one. It's just my style, and I'm afraid that I've gotten too set in my ways to change."

"Well, all right," Katie said, sounding disappointed. She gave me Donna's address and phone number in the small town of

Selkirk and then said she would telephone her and tell her to expect my call.

I figured a schoolteacher wouldn't be home until later in the afternoon, so I waited until 5:30 to call. She picked up after several rings.

"This is Archie Goodwin," I said.

"Oh yes, Mr. Goodwin, Katie Padgett told me that I would be hearing from you," Donna Newman said in a soft voice. "She said that you wanted to come and see me, although I'm not sure there is anything that I can tell you about my uncle's death that can't be discussed over the telephone."

"You may very well be right, Miss Newman, but I always prefer to talk face-to-face."

"May I ask what your interest is in my uncle's death?"

"Of course you may. There are people that knew your uncle who are questioning whether he committed suicide."

"Why, that is just ridiculous," Donna said, her voice rising hoarsely. "Who in the world would want to kill Uncle Logan?"

"That is precisely what I am trying to find out, Miss Newman."

"That police chief, Blankenship, and the coroner's inquest, both have determined that my uncle killed himself. Isn't that proof enough?"

"Suicide is of course a possibility, but I know you loved your uncle. Wouldn't you want to know if there was some likelihood that he was murdered?"

A long pause at the other end, followed by a deep breath. "Oh, I suppose so. Katie tells me you are a private detective from New York City, Mr. Goodwin."

"Guilty as charged."

"So I assume you must have a client who is paying you to investigate my uncle's death."

"Not guilty this time, Miss Newman. I am undertaking what you would call a pro bono investigation."

"Well, I still think that my uncle ended his own life, and I really don't know why anybody would think otherwise."

"You may be right, but I would still like to come out there and talk to you. I promise not to take too much of your time."

She took a few seconds to respond. "Well . . . all right," she finally said without enthusiasm. "When were you planning to be here?"

"Tonight, if you have no objection. You know the roads around here better than I do. How long would it take me to get to your place?"

"No more than a half hour. There are only very small towns on the road between where you are and Selkirk. Do you have my address?"

"Yes, I got it from Katie Padgett."

"You should have no trouble finding the little house that I rent," she said, giving me directions. "When do you expect to be here?"

"Would eight o'clock be all right with you?"

"Yes, I should be done grading papers by then."

After one of Mrs. Goodwin's fine dinners—Yankee pot roast with potatoes and carrots—I set off for the town of Selkirk, which I vaguely remembered and which, according to my mother, was still "something of a wide spot in the highway." Heading west into the late June evening sunset, I passed through small burgs I hadn't seen in decades, although they looked like they hadn't *changed* in decades either.

Selkirk was no exception. Its one-block business district consisted of tired two-story brick buildings and storefronts crying out for tenants. The only bit of brightness along that commercial stretch was a red-and-blue neon sign in the window of a bar advertising a national brand of beer.

I turned onto the residential street where Donna Newman lived and had no trouble locating her house, a small frame bungalow with a bright red front door. After parking at the curb, I went up the short brick sidewalk and rang the bell.

That red door swung open, and I was greeted by a curly-haired and well-proportioned young blond woman who could not have been more than an inch over five feet, even in heels. Her smile was reserved and her blue eyes were lidded. "You are Mr. Goodwin?"

"I am, and you are Miss Newman, I assume?" I replied, giving her what Lily Rowan has called my winsome grin.

With a still-reserved smile, she let me in, directed me to a small but neat living room, and gestured me to a sofa.

"I hope you like tea; I just brewed some," she said with what seemed to be a touch of pride.

I don't happen to like the stuff, but in the interest of civility, I told her I would have some. She left, presumably in the direction of the kitchen, and came back carrying two cups of tea, setting one of them on the end table beside me.

"Milk or sugar?" she asked, and I replied that I prefer it black, which in this case was preferable to saying I don't like tea at all.

After she eased herself into a chair at right angles to me, Donna stirred her tea nervously and looked up, trying without success to smile. "I find this very uncomfortable, Mr. Goodwin," she said. "I agreed to see you, but now that you are here, I realize that I have almost nothing to say. I really do think that my great-uncle must have killed himself, because I cannot imagine why anyone would want him dead."

"I respect your opinion, Miss Newman," I said, taking a sip of the brew and avoiding making a face. "Assuming for argument's sake that he did kill himself, what do you think was the reason?"

Now it was her turn to drink tea, possibly preparing her answer. "I don't believe Uncle Logan ever got over Aunt Sylvia's death. Oh, he put up a great front all right, but as you may be aware, I visited him regularly, at least once a week, and I could tell that he was just never the same after my aunt died."

"Talk to me a little bit about yourself," I asked, knowing from past experience that getting a person to tell something relating to his or her life can be both flattering and a way of loosening up that individual. And I could sense from Donna Newman's bearing and worried expression that she definitely needed some loosening up.

"Well, I'm an Ohio native and grew up down in the little town of Waverly, if you know where that is."

"I do, but only vaguely. I came from this part of the country, too, years ago now, although I don't get back here very often."

"Well, anyway," Donna continued, "my parents still live in Waverly. My father is a veterinarian and my mother teaches courses in French and Spanish at the high school, which is probably why I got into teaching. I grew up around it."

"So off to college you went?"

"Yes, to Ohio University in Athens. And after graduation, I came straight here and began teaching English. I've been at the high school just down the street for two years now."

"Isn't Athens where Katie Padgett went, too, and at about the same time?"

"Oh, I wouldn't be at all surprised," she said offhandedly. "It's a big place, and they've got a good journalism program, which she probably was a part of."

"Tell me how you and Logan Mulgrew were related," I asked.

"Technically, I was not related to Uncle Logan, at least not by blood. I am the granddaughter of a man named Lester Newman," Donna said, "and his sister was dear Aunt Sylvia, who was really my great-aunt and who, as you know, was married to Uncle Logan."

"Were your grandfather and your aunt close?"

"Very. When Sylvia died, Lester was as broken up as if she had been his wife, rather than his sister. The family bond was extremely strong."

"Where is your grandfather now?"

"He's also back in Waverly, although he does not live with my folks. He has been a widower for many years and is retired as a postal carrier. Life has not been very good to him. He saw a lot of action and won medals in the Second World War, even though he was quite a bit older than other servicemen. He's never been quite the same since the war. Doctors called his problem 'battle fatigue.'"

"I'm sorry to hear that. Back to Logan Mulgrew. Do you have any sense of how people in town felt about him?"

Donna took another sip of her tea. "Well, I know that he was highly respected. After all, he had been the town's leading banker for . . . oh, I don't know how many years, but since long before I was born."

"Can you think of any enemies your uncle might have had?"

She shook her head. "Not really, although he never talked to me about his business or any other relationships when I visited him."

"Did your grandfather like him?"

"I don't think the subject ever came up in my conversations with either one of them," Donna said. "Surely you are not suggesting that my grandfather would have reason to dislike Uncle Logan."

"I'm not suggesting anything, Miss Newman. Does the name Harold Mapes mean anything to you?"

"No, should it?"

"Perhaps not. He was a dairy farmer who had borrowed money from your uncle's bank some years back and couldn't keep up with the payments, so he got foreclosed on and ended up losing his farm. He has never forgiven Logan Mulgrew for this and publicly said some very threatening things about him."

"Well, I am certainly sorry for what happened to Mr.—what was it?—Mapes, but after all, banks are businesses," Donna replied. "You have got to abide by their rules."

"I can't disagree with you there, but I mention this episode to point out that your uncle did have what might be called enemies."

"Maybe *an* enemy," she said sharply. "That can happen to anyone who is in business."

"You may not like what I am going to say, but Mapes wasn't the only one who said threatening things about your uncle. There's Eldon Kiefer, whose daughter worked as a secretary at the bank."

"Kiefer? I don't recognize that name."

"His daughter is Becky."

"Oh yes! I met Becky once when I visited Uncle Logan at the bank, but I never knew her last name. She seemed shy but very pleasant."

"Apparently your uncle thought so, too. There was talk that they had a relationship that may have resulted in a pregnancy."

"I really do not have to listen to that kind of talk!" Donna said, standing and putting her hands on her hips. "I am going to have to ask you to leave, Mr. Goodwin. I don't know what your game is, but I don't like it one bit."

"You should be aware of what is being said about your uncle," I responded, getting to my feet. "And you need to know that Kiefer also threatened him."

"And what has happened to dear Becky?" she said bitterly.

"She works at a bank in Cleveland."

"And what became of her so-called pregnancy?" Donna demanded.

"That I don't know."

"Hah! It sounds to me like the young woman was trying to pull a fast one and get money out of my uncle for something she did with someone else. Or are you just trying to generate a case where none exists?"

"Whatever you may think of me, I do not operate that way, Miss Newman. Do you know anything about Carrie Yeager?" I asked, pushing my luck.

"Just what is that supposed to mean?"

"She was the caregiver to your great-aunt during her last days, wasn't she?"

"Yes . . . that is true . . ." Donna replied, caution creeping into her tone. "I only met her maybe a half-dozen times. She was not always around when I went to visit Aunt Sylvia."

"What was your opinion of her?"

"She seemed . . . I don't know, somewhat off-center, I would say."

"Meaning?"

"Meaning she was kind of vague and dreamy and unfocused each time I met her."

"Were you comfortable having her look after your aunt?"

She frowned. "I guess I'm just not sure about that."

"How did she get along with your great-uncle?"

Donna raised her shoulders and let them drop. "All right, I guess. Why are you asking?"

"Just my native curiosity," I said. I briefly considered bringing up Lester Newman's suspicion involving Mulgrew's relationship with Carrie Yeager and also his suspicion that the banker may have poisoned his wife, but I knew I had worn out my welcome in this quaint little house in this not-so-quaint little town. "Thank you for seeing me, Miss Newman," I said. "And the tea was very good."

Hands still on hips, an unsmiling Donna did not reply and gestured toward the door with her eyes. I got the none-too-subtle message and dipped my chin, then walked out into the night, wondering if I should have handled the visit differently.

CHAPTER 10

I had just gotten back to my mother's house when the telephone jangled. "Yes, yes, he's here," she said into the instrument. "You are coming over now? Well . . . all right, yes."

"That was Tom Blankenship," my mother said after hanging up. "He wants to see you about something, but he didn't say what."

"I've got an idea why he wants to talk," I said, and it turned out I was right. Within fifteen minutes, the bell rang, and Mom swung open the door to the local police chief.

"Please come in, Chief Blankenship," she said. "If you and Archie need to talk, I will leave you alone while I putter in the kitchen."

"No, stay with us, Mom," I said. "Anything the gentleman needs to discuss with me can be done in your presence."

Blankenship stepped in, looking resplendent in his dark blue uniform and wearing an expression that showed uncertainty as to how to proceed.

"Please have a seat," my mother said, "and I will get some coffee for all of us. I already have some in the pot."

Our visitor looked uncomfortable as he and I sat facing each other. "I am not sure how to say this, Mr. Goodwin," Blankenship began, "but a half hour or so ago, I received a telephone call from Donna Newman over in Selkirk. She said that you had just visited her."

"That is correct," I told him.

"She said that your visit upset her very much," the chief went on, "and she complained to me about it. She told me you subjected her to an interrogation."

"Such was not my intent, and I would not term our talk an interrogation. I merely discussed individuals who had occasion to dislike her late uncle."

At this point, my mother reentered the room and set cups of coffee on the end tables next to us, taking a seat herself.

The chief nodded his thanks and continued. "Based on what Miss Newman told me, it appears that you are conducting an investigation into Logan Mulgrew's death. Is that true, Mr. Goodwin?"

"I think it is fair to say that questions remain as to whether or not Mr. Mulgrew's death was caused by a self-inflicted wound."

Blankenship took a sip of coffee, preparing his response as the tension in the room heightened. "Mr. Goodwin, I am keenly aware that you are a well-known private investigator in New York. But this is not New York, and we here do not take kindly to outside interference in our enforcement of the law."

"I understand, Chief Blankenship. Is there any doubt in your mind as to who pulled the trigger on the gun whose bullet killed Logan Mulgrew?"

"None whatsoever," the chief said.

"Is it fair to say that not everyone agrees with you?" I responded.

Blankenship's face reddened. "If you are referring to that young newspaperwoman, I am well aware of her opinion, which I take issue with."

"What about the gunshot that was fired through Miss Padgett's apartment window?"

"I have already made it clear that I believe that was caused by someone who in all likelihood was inebriated and was unwisely and rashly letting off steam. And if you are wondering if the gun that killed Mr. Mulgrew was the same one that fired the shot into Miss Padgett's apartment, the answer is no. Mr. Mulgrew died of a shot fired from a .38-caliber revolver, while we dug a .32-caliber shell out of the wall of Miss Padgett's apartment."

"Is gunfire in town a common occurrence here?"

The chief inhaled deeply. "I haven't seen it before in the years I've been on the force, but that does not mean that it can't happen."

"Sure, anything can happen, of course," I said, "but doesn't it seem unusual to you that the shot got fired into—of all places in town—the reporter's residence so soon after her article ran in the *Trumpet* raising questions about Mulgrew's death?"

It was obvious Tom Blankenship was growing frustrated with the direction the conversation had taken, but I was not about to let up. "Years ago, my boss, Nero Wolfe, taught me to be suspicious of coincidences, and I have to say that I'm darned suspicious of this one. Were any other shots fired around town that night?"

"Not that I am aware of," the tight-lipped chief said. "Mr. Goodwin, I cannot stop you from looking into Mr. Mulgrew's death, as long as you don't get in the way of any police investigations."

"With all due respect, I am not aware of any current police investigation into the death of Logan Mulgrew. Unless, of course, I am uninformed as to your department's activities. If there is indeed an investigation, I stand corrected."

"I make it a general policy not to comment upon ongoing operations, so I am afraid I am not at liberty to say anything more," Blankenship replied, rising.

"Now I am well aware that Miss Newman is not a resident of this community, and therefore is outside of our jurisdiction, so I cannot protect her if you choose to submit her to a further inquisition. And you also are not a resident of this community, for that matter. Mrs. Goodwin, thank you for your hospitality. Good evening to you both," Blankenship said as he put on his cap, bowed slightly, did an about-face, and left.

"I hope that little discussion of ours did not disturb you too much," I said to my mother as she shut the front door behind the departing and somewhat stiff policeman.

"Quite the contrary," she said with a smile. "I found it fascinating to watch you at work, something I had never seen."

"I'm not sure how much work I really did just now."

"Archie, you may not think so, but I happen to be pretty good at reading situations, and I could see that Chief Blankenship was more than a little impressed with you, however much he might be reluctant to admit it. Your mention of Mr. Wolfe further showed him that you are someone who has got to be reckoned with."

"That really wasn't the reason I brought Wolfe's name up."

"Oh, I know that," my mother said. "You have never been one to show off. I just hope you don't run into some sort of danger digging around in the affairs of the late Mr. Mulgrew."

"*Affairs* would seem to be an apt word, all right, if what has been said about Mulgrew has any truth to it," I said as the phone rang. My mother answered, cupped the receiver, and whispered

"Katie Padgett" to me, and I nodded. "Yes, he is here," she said, handing me the instrument.

"Hi, Archie, I was just calling to see how your meeting with Donna went."

"It could have been better. She wasn't in the least bit happy with my questions and comments, and she made sure that your police chief knew about it."

"I'm sorry to hear that. As I said before, she is really a very nice person."

"Which means the fault probably was mine," I told her. "That would not be the first time in my life. Anyway, I wouldn't invite the two of us to the same party."

"I'll phone her, Archie, and try to smooth things over," Katie said as we ended the call.

"Say, do you happen to know which local garage Charles Purcell works at?" I asked my mother.

"Oh, Archie, you've really got your teeth into this business, haven't you? Yes, I know where Mr. Purcell works. It's Renson's, on Maple Street just a little over a block west of the courthouse. At least that's where he was the last time I heard, which was a few months back."

"Can you describe him?"

"He's short, and I would call him stout, or at least stocky, although nowhere near the size of Nero Wolfe. And he's pretty close to bald. He wears glasses and doesn't have a mustache or beard, or at least he didn't the last time I saw him."

"Well, it just so happens that on my drive down here from New York, I noticed a rattle coming from somewhere in the rear end of the convertible. Now I don't know much about cars, but it would seem likely that Charles Purcell does. What do you think I should do about that doggone rattle I've got?"

"I think that first thing tomorrow morning, you should drive straight over to Renson's Garage and hope that Mr. Purcell is on duty and can fix that rattle of yours."

"You have read my mind, which you have been doing for so many years!" I said.

CHAPTER 11

Renson's Garage occupied a single-story, ivy-covered brick building that I vaguely remembered from my childhood. It doubled as a filling station with gas pumps in front and had two bays for auto repairs. I pulled up in front and walked into the small office, which was unoccupied.

"Be with you in a minute," a voice called out from one of the bays. In fact, it was less than a minute when a chunky, balding man in coveralls stepped in with a questioning look. Being the perceptive detective that I am, I recognized him from my mother's description. And it did not hurt that the word *Charles* was stitched in red on the front of his soiled coveralls.

"I'm getting a rattling sound somewhere in the rear of my car," I told him, gesturing toward the dusty convertible that sat in front.

"I've got nothing urgent going on here right now, so let's take a look," he said, wiping off his hands with a rag that he kept in his back pocket. "I'll drive her on in and put her up on the rack, okay?"

"Fine by me," I replied, handing him the car keys. Less than a minute later, the car was inside and off the ground, as the two of us looked up at it, one of whom knew what he was doing. Purcell played the beam of his flashlight around the car's undercarriage, then nodded. "Aha," he said, winking at me and nodding.

"What is the verdict, Doctor? Will the patient survive?"

"Oh, I think so. See right there?" he said as he held the flashlight steady.

"To be honest, I'm not sure what I'm looking at."

"A loose bolt, that's what. Nothing that would likely have caused an accident, but still, it needs to be tightened up or you'd have to live with the rattling, which would have gotten a lot worse when the bolt finally fell off."

"I'll bet you've looked at the underbellies of a lot of automobiles in your time."

"Enough," Purcell said with a scowl. "This is not how I figured I would end up, but it's the hand that I've been dealt. I don't think I've seen you around here before, have I? I noticed you've got New York plates, something of a rarity in these parts."

"I'm visiting family in town. I grew up here a long time ago."

"I think that I've been here too long myself," the banker-turned-mechanic said.

"Well, you seem to know your way around cars, so mark me down as impressed. I know enough to turn the key in the ignition, and that's about the extent of it."

Purcell snorted as he stood under the convertible and tightened the errant bolt with a wrench. "It's a good thing I do, because my previous career crashed and burned, in a way."

"I'm sorry to hear that."

"Not half as sorry as I am," Purcell said bitterly, shaking his head.

"If you don't mind my asking, what was your previous career?"

"No, I don't mind your asking. Everybody in town knows all about it. I had been in banking since I got out of school—that's right, an auto mechanic with an actual college degree—two degrees, in fact. Anyway, I had worked my way up in a couple of banks around the state and felt like I had gotten to know the business pretty well. So . . . I got the bright idea to open my own bank, and right here."

"And why not, since you had already gotten experience in the world of finance?"

"I found out why not," Purcell said as he hit the switch that lowered the convertible gently to the garage floor. "Somebody didn't like having competition and made damned sure that I failed."

"Sounds to me like there was some dirty business involved."

"You could call it that. I found out just how easy it is to start a rumor, or maybe calling what happened a whispering campaign is more accurate."

"So I'm to take from your experience that not all bankers are upright pillars of the community?"

That brought a mirthless laugh from Purcell. "That is a fair statement, Mr. . . . ?"

"Goodwin, Archie Goodwin."

"Well, Mr. Goodwin, there was a man here who had a bank that he had owned and run for many years. It had been the only bank in town for decades, and he was determined to keep it that way."

"Had anyone else tried to open another bank here before?"

"Not that I am aware of, at least not in recent times, certainly not since the Depression. This area has experienced at least modest population growth in the last few years, and there is certainly room for more than a single bank now."

"But one individual doesn't think so?"

"*Didn't* think so. That individual, Logan Mulgrew by name, is dead. If I told you I was sorry about that, I would be lying."

"Oh yeah, Mulgrew. I heard that he killed himself, didn't he?"

"Uh . . . so I've also heard. Say, your name is Goodwin, right?"

"It is."

"If I remember right, a woman by that name opened an account in my bank."

"You remember right. That would be my mother, who lives in a farmhouse out on the Portsmouth Road. I'm here visiting her."

"Well, please thank her for me, will you? I wish there had been more people like her. I believe she did get her money back when we had to close our doors, didn't she?"

"That's my understanding. Just how did this Mulgrew put you out of business?"

"The rumor mill and the power of suggestion are both alive and well in this town, Mr. Goodwin," Purcell said. "And Logan Mulgrew knew just how to manipulate them. Oh, he was subtle, at least in the beginning, when he pointed out in casual conversations to his customers and anyone else in hearing distance how well funded and insured his institution was.

"Then he began to send out inserts with his customers' monthly statements that carried a headline reading 'Bank Where Your Dollars Are Safe,' along with text that specified how well protected money was at Farmer's State Bank & Trust. Never mind that at my own bank, the money was just as safe and just as highly insured."

"Nasty piece of business," I remarked.

"Yeah, and it got nastier," Purcell said as he pulled off his work gloves. "Mulgrew then started a whispering campaign to the effect that it was just a matter of time before my bank would close down. Many of those people who had opened accounts with me rushed in to withdraw their money."

"Shades of the kind of runs on banks that were common back in the Depression," I remarked.

"That's exactly right, Mr. Goodwin. I managed to get everyone their dough, but I was wiped out, ruined, in the process. I had to sell my house, and my life fell apart. Oh hell, you don't need to listen to this tale of woe. I leave that to my fellow drinkers in the bar where I hang out. We all cry on one another's shoulders, for a variety of reasons."

"Sounds like you have plenty of cause to beef. Why do you think Mulgrew killed himself?"

Purcell paused several beats before answering. "I really couldn't say," he replied with a finality that sent the clear message that our conversation was at an end.

When I asked how much I owed him, he said a sawbuck would cover it. I handed him the money and we shook hands briefly, then I drove off as he stood in the entrance to the bay, hands on hips and wearing a grim expression.

CHAPTER 12

"Well, were you able to see Charles Purcell?" my mother asked when I returned to the house.

"Yes, and he made the relatively small repair to the car, which it needed. He is a very bitter man."

"He has much to be bitter about, Archie, as I told you. Did he talk about his problems?"

"He did, at some length, but he really clammed up when I asked if he had any idea why Mulgrew might have killed himself. Also, and you will be interested in this, I told him my name and he remembered that a Goodwin was among the people who opened accounts with his ill-fated bank.

"I said you were my mother, and he told me he hoped you'd gotten all your money back. I reassured him that you had."

"It was very thoughtful of him to remember. I have heard—from Edna, of course—that Mr. Purcell spends a lot of time now in a local tavern."

"He did make reference to that and said he and some of the other regulars commiserate about their problems. Not a very healthy way to go through life."

"And he has no wife to go home to anymore. He can't be a very cheerful presence in the home of his son and daughter-in-law. Now I will ask you the very same question that you posed to me soon after you arrived here: Do you think Charles Purcell might have killed Logan Mulgrew?"

"I wouldn't reject the idea. I have a little more trouble, though, imagining him firing a shot through the window of Katie Padgett's apartment. Somehow, he doesn't seem like the type, although I can't tell you why."

"I would hate to think of him, or anyone else, for that matter, doing such a thing."

Shifting gears, I asked: "Can you picture that dairy farmer, Harold Mapes, as a murderer?"

"Really, Archie, I don't really even know the man. Oh, I did meet him twice or maybe three times, each time in our church. He and his wife attended for a while, and then they stopped coming, probably because of their embarrassment at having lost the farm and their inability to keep up their financial pledge to the church. Mrs. Mapes, her name is Emily, seemed very nice, but is extremely reserved. My impression is that he does most of the talking for both of them."

"Where is the farm they work as tenants?"

"On this very road, Archie, about six miles south of here. It's a beautifully maintained place with a two-story white frame house with a bay window set in a grove of oak trees and two barns, both recently painted. Are you thinking of visiting Mr. Mapes?"

"The thought has occurred to me."

"And just what do you hope to accomplish in such a visit?" asked my ever-practical mother.

"I am not sure. Nero Wolfe has said that when I have an itch, I need to scratch it."

"And you have got an itch?"

I nodded.

"Would it do any good if I told you to be careful?"

"It might. Do you feel that Harold Mapes is the violent type?"

"Well, as you already know, he is certainly the angry type, at least as far as the subject of Logan Mulgrew is concerned."

"With good reason. It seems fair to say that Mulgrew cost him his livelihood."

"I have an idea, Archie."

That got my attention. Whenever my mother used those words, *I have an idea*, when I was a kid, it usually meant that she was about to propose something that would pose a challenge for me, like spending more time on my homework or raking leaves or washing the car. "What is your idea?" I asked, having no clue as to where this was headed.

"As I mentioned, the Mapes couple attended our church sometime back and then stopped. We now have a program where we take a basket of fruit to those who have drifted away for whatever reason."

"Ah, the laying on of a Christian guilt trip."

"No, not at all, Archie. None of us who take these baskets ever say anything like 'We would like to see you back in church again.' Rather, we ask if there is anything at all we can do for them or anyone they would like us to pray for."

"And how has that worked out?"

"A few whom we've called on have returned to Sunday services, at least on occasion, although that is not the main reason for our visits. We really want to be seen as a caring community."

"Put me down as impressed, Mom. And as you well know, I am not a churchgoer."

"I am very aware of that," she replied with just a touch of resignation. "But back to my idea. I believe a basket of fruit is in order for the Mapes family, and you and I should be the ones to deliver it."

"You want *me* to go along?"

"And why not? There is something particularly neighborly about a mother and her adult son calling upon some neighbors. And, if we are fortunate, both Mrs. Mapes and her husband will be present. It will give you the opportunity to size up the man in a nonthreatening situation."

"Maybe they will beware of Greeks bearing gifts, as it were."

"I don't think so, and our basket of fruit can hardly be mistaken for a Trojan horse. But we won't know until we've tried, will we?" my mother said with irrefutable logic.

"Point well taken. All right, I'm game for this approach. After all, I don't have a better idea."

Wanting to be as much help as I could, I drove my mother to a local grocery store, where she bought a variety of fruits—oranges, apples, peaches, pears, and two kinds of grapes. We then stopped at a dime store and bought a basket.

"You really didn't have to drive me around, Archie. I am still quite capable behind the wheel," my mother said after we had arrived at home and she began to assemble the fruit basket.

"Oh, I know that, but I felt I should do my part on this project," I said. "When do you suggest we visit the Mapes family?"

"Tomorrow morning, about ten o'clock. In the past, that's when I've been most successful at finding people home."

CHAPTER 13

So it was that the next morning, my mother and I ventured forth on a mission with mixed goals: Christian fellowship and an ongoing death investigation. I drove south on the Portsmouth Road until my mother said, "It's coming up on the left, Archie. There's the grove of oak trees I mentioned."

The farm buildings looked prosperous. The white house with green shutters and a bay window was set well back from the road, nestled in those trees, and two big red barns were flanked by smaller outbuildings.

I drove in on a blacktop drive neatly edged with bricks and pulled up close to the front entrance. We got out, my mother carrying the fruit basket, and before we could get to the bell, the door swung open.

A gray-haired woman of middle age looked over rimless glasses at us, her face a question mark.

"Hello, Mrs. Mapes, I am Marjorie Goodwin, from the Presbyterian church in town. You may not remember me."

"Oh yes," the woman said, slowly breaking into a dimpled smile. "Of course I remember; you were the very first person to greet us when we were at the church that first time, and you made us feel so welcome. Please do come in."

"This is my son, Archie," Mom said. "He just happened to be in town visiting me, and I asked him to come along."

"I am happy to see you both," our hostess said, gesturing us through an entrance hall and into a sun-filled living room with two large windows on its south wall and that bay window on the west. "Please sit down. Would you care for some coffee?"

We both said we would, and Mrs. Mapes left for the kitchen. She must have opened a back door, because I could hear her calling to the outside, "Harold, come on in, we have some guests."

Before she returned with the coffee, a tall, lean man with white hair falling over one eye stepped in and looked at us with his own questioning expression. My mother explained who we were, and he nodded.

"Yeah, I do remember meeting you at the church. That was a while back," he said, easing into a chair. "I believe Emily is bringing coffee. And I'm here to tell you that she makes good coffee," he added, tugging at the collar of his blue work shirt.

"We hope you both have been well, and we've brought some fruit, although I wouldn't be surprised if you may grow some of your own, at least apples," my mother said, handing him the basket.

He took it gingerly just as Emily Mapes returned carrying a tray with four coffee cups. "There's always a pot brewing here," she said as she served each of us. "Harold can't live without it, or so he tells me."

"We're happy to find you both at home and hope you are doing well," my mother said.

"We are, Mrs. Goodwin, thank you," Emily replied. "I am afraid I'm embarrassed to say that we haven't been to church for some time now. Life on a farm can be very busy, and . . ."

"No need whatever to be embarrassed or to explain," Mom said, waving away the spoken concern with a hand. "It's just that we at the church have missed you and wanted you to have this little expression of our affection. Whenever you are able to come back, you would be most welcome."

"Things here can get a little hectic sometimes," Mapes said, directing his comment at me. "I don't believe you're from these parts, are you?"

"No, I live in New York and am visiting my mother for a few days. It's nice to get away from the city sometimes."

"By golly, it's been at least a dozen years since I've been to New York, and that was only for a couple of days when I got mustered out of the Marines. I saw service in the Pacific during the war and got wounded at Okinawa, although not badly. It was pure hell on that island, though. Were you in the service?"

"Army," I said. "I spent most of my time in Washington."

"I would've gladly traded places with you," Mapes said with a wry grin, "but I know that everybody had a part to play. Did you have to work in that big Pentagon building they built during the war?"

"Only briefly, I'm happy to report. Say, I'm not a farmer, but I must tell you that I'm impressed with what I've seen of your spread."

Mapes nodded curtly. "I'm happy to show you around, if you care to."

"I'd like that, if the ladies will excuse us," I said.

"You two go ahead," Emily Mapes said. "It's such a nice day to be outside. We will just stay in here and chat."

I followed Mapes out through the kitchen to the back door. "None of my crew are here today," he said as we stepped outside. "I milked the cows alone this morning, and I'll do it again tonight, but that's okay; it's not all that hard now with milking machines. But they'll be back tomorrow."

"How many do you have working here?"

"Two, and the three of us are enough to handle everything except at harvest time, when I bring in some others," he said as we walked out to one of the barns. "Just so that you know, I don't own this farm, I wish I did. I work it as a tenant for a very rich man who lives out of town."

"Maybe you can buy it from him sometime," I suggested.

"Hah! That is not very damned likely," he said. "Maybe you don't know this, but I had a spread of my own at one time, and I lost it because of . . . well, I lost it."

"Because of what? Or if you'd prefer not to say, I would understand."

"No, I don't care," Mapes said, brushing back the errant shock of hair from his forehead. "Everybody around here knows about it anyway. I couldn't keep up the payments on my own farm and . . . well, it got foreclosed on."

"That had to be a bitter pill," I said as we walked into a barn and Mapes leaned on a green-and-yellow tractor, rubbing a hand along the gleaming chassis as if caressing it.

"Bitter, yeah. I heard somebody say once that lawyers are the meanest people in the world. Well, Mr. Goodwin, they're wrong; it's bankers, those sons of bitches. Or at least one banker, who . . . oh, never mind. My wife says that I've become too damned sour."

"It sounds to me like you have good reason."

"Maybe, but I've got to learn to quit griping. Besides, one thing turned out okay."

"What's that?"

"The bastard who foreclosed on me, well . . . he'll never fore-close on anybody else again," Mapes said.

"How so?"

"He's dead, that's how so."

"Oh, wait. Are you talking about that Logan Mulgrew? I heard that he shot himself."

"He's dead, that counts for something, anyway."

"Do you think it was a suicide?"

"That I couldn't say," Mapes replied, his expression grim. "Let me show you the milking shed." This was a low building a short distance from the barn we had been in. There wasn't much to look at, as the cows were not in it, but were, as I was to learn, out in a pasture grazing.

"We milk sixty Holsteins in here, twice every day. Using the machines, it goes a lot faster than back in the old days, when it was all done by hand."

"I don't know a lot about cows, but my father was a farmer. I do remember that the Holsteins are the black-and-white ones, right?"

"Yep, and they give the most milk of any breed. Well, I sup-pose we should get back to the ladies."

"Thanks for the little tour. This is quite an operation."

Mapes did not respond. Since Mulgrew came up in the dis-cussion the farmer had become sullen, and I was not about to bring up the man again.

CHAPTER 14

"Well, what did you think of Mr. Mapes?" my mother asked when we were in the car on our way home.

"Bitter, by his own admission. And far from regretful over the demise of one Logan Mulgrew."

"Do you think Mr. Mapes had anything to do with that demise, Archie?"

"I would like to be able to give you a definitive answer, but I can't. Do you know if Mulgrew ever foreclosed on any other farmers?"

"I don't, but I suppose it wouldn't be surprising. We had a couple of bad farming years a while back."

"Yes, I remember that you wrote me about it at the time."

"There is no reason I would have heard about any other foreclosures. I think that when that happens, most people are so embarrassed they try to keep it quiet. The reason I knew about the Mapes situation was that he was so public in his anger toward Mulgrew."

"Well, it's obvious that anger hasn't gone away," I said. "The man is seething just below the surface, like a volcano ready to erupt."

"Or is it possible that he already has erupted?" my mother asked.

"Say, there could be a place for you in the detective business. You have just the right amount of skepticism, or is it cynicism? I can never get those two straight, but don't tell Wolfe. He is forever critiquing my grammar and usage."

"You poor thing. And yet you always got good grades in school."

"Yeah, but I never had an English teacher who was as much of a stickler as Nero Wolfe, although you corrected me at home on occasion."

"That does not seem to have scarred you emotionally."

"I've learned to live with it," I said as we returned to my mother's home. No sooner were we inside than the telephone began ringing. "It's for you," Mom said, again cupping the phone. "Katie Padgett."

"Hi, Archie," she said when I was on the line. "I'm wondering what, if anything, you've been able to find out."

"Not a lot. I have spent a little time with both Purcell and Mapes, but I can't say I've learned much other than to find them both angry."

"About Mulgrew, of course."

"Of course. And what have you found out since we last talked?"

"I've got a lead on where Carrie Yeager is."

"Really?"

"Yes, I finally used the brain I was given and talked to the woman who oversees the apartment building downtown that Carrie moved into after Mulgrew died. I told her that I was a friend of Carrie's and needed to get hold of her because she had left some of her clothes and other personal items with me. It turns out Carrie had given the woman her forwarding address, which I had hoped. She's living in Charleston, West Virginia, now, and I have the address."

"Any idea why Charleston?"

"No, but she sure left this town quietly. I've been doing a lot of thinking about Carrie lately, and I'm wondering if we haven't overlooked her as a suspect."

"Why would she have wanted to kill Mulgrew, Katie?"

"I don't know. Maybe she hoped that he would marry her or at least leave her a nice chunk of his fortune, the latter of which didn't happen from what I've heard."

"I've also heard that Miss Yeager did not get anything from the Mulgrew estate," I said. "But presuming she knew she wasn't included in the will, what good would it do her to kill him?"

"As was once written, 'Hell hath no fury like a woman scorned,'" Katie said.

"I've heard that line, too, but I have to wonder if Carrie Yeager's fury, if that's indeed what it was, would have been enough to drive her to murder," I observed.

"Maybe not, but don't you think that it would be worthwhile to go down to Charleston?"

"Will your paper send you down there on assignment?"

"Not those cheapskates, Archie. But I am owed some time, and my editors don't have to know what I do with my days off."

"All in the interest of surprising your bosses with a scoop, right?"

"Could be. Are you game?"

"Why not? It's not that long a drive. Any idea if Miss Yeager has gotten herself a job in Charleston?"

"No, but I have a feeling that it won't be that hard to find out. Have you ever been to Charleston before?" Katie asked.

"We passed through it once when I was a kid. My father had entered his prize bull in a competition at the West Virginia State Fair, which is somewhere farther down in that state. He thought he'd have a better chance than at Ohio's fair, which is much larger."

"Did he win?"

"The bull took a second-place ribbon in its category, which was a damn sight better than it would have done up in Columbus, so I guess you could call it a successful trip. I recall that my father was unusually happy on the drive back home."

"That's better than my memory of West Virginia," Katie said. "As a family, we took a driving vacation down there when I was in grade school, and it poured buckets with thunder and lightning for three solid days. We couldn't go horseback riding or hiking or even canoeing."

"Well, if you are serious about going to Charleston, we could do it tomorrow. There's no rain in the forecast."

"Sounds good, and it will give me a chance to see a real live detective at work."

"Try to contain your excitement," I told her.

CHAPTER 15

"So you and this Katie of yours are going off to Charleston on what may be a wild goose chase," my mother said at breakfast the next day in a less-than-enthusiastic tone.

"First off, Mom, she's not 'this Katie of mine' by any stretch. But you may be right that we are off on a fool's errand."

"Well, I would be a liar if I told you I wasn't interested in learning just what the Yeager woman may be up to. I'm afraid I am getting to be like my sister."

"You don't have to worry about that happening, Mom. You and Aunt Edna are poles apart, I'm happy to say."

At 8:30, I swung by the building where Katie Padgett lived, and she was standing at the curb wearing a summery yellow dress, sandals, and a smile.

"Right on time, Archie!" she chirped, stepping gracefully into the convertible. "I came downstairs less than a minute ago."

"That's the window that got broken by a gunshot, right?" I asked, pointing up at the second floor over Mason's hardware store.

"That's the one, and the scary thing is, I had been standing by that window just a minute or so earlier."

"Lucky timing on your part," I said as we pulled away and began our jaunt southeast toward Charleston.

"I've wanted to get you alone for some time," Katie said.

"Uh-oh."

"Oh, it's nothing like that, silly," she said, punching my right shoulder playfully. "I want to hear about some of the cases you and Nero Wolfe have worked on. It must be such an exciting life."

"On occasion that's true, but much of the time, it's me hunting down people or clues in my dogged and plodding fashion and delivering what—or who—I find to Mr. Wolfe, the brains of the operation, and he invariably figures the whole thing out." I proceeded to tell her about the gun battle in our office with Wolfe getting shot in the arm while sitting at his desk and me then plugging the shooter.* And also my narrow escape from that angry bull in the Upstate New York meadow.

"I love your story about the bull. It sounds like you've had some pretty wild times."

"Not really. I just gave you a couple of exceptions to what is a generally unexciting life. And gunplay rarely enters into the picture. Now it's time for you to tell me what you plan to do once we locate our Miss Yeager."

Katie laid out her scheme, and I was impressed with its structure, if not its integrity. But then, I've been known to play fast and loose with facts myself when interviewing suspects and

---

* *The Rubber Band* by Rex Stout, 1936

cajoling them into making a visit to Nero Wolfe in the brownstone. After further discussion of the approach to be taken with Carrie Yeager, we crossed the Ohio River into West Virginia and were greeted by a welcome center with a pole that was flying what I assumed to be the state flag.

"Why are we stopping here?" Katie asked as I pulled into the center's parking lot.

"To get a map of Charleston," I told her. "I don't relish the idea of driving aimlessly around town looking for an address."

"Of course, I should have thought of that," my passenger said in an abashed tone as she gave me Carrie Yeager's address.

"Shouldn't be too hard to find her," I said after I brought a map back to the car and studied it. "I see that her street is just a few blocks from the capitol."

"Which happens to be the tallest building in West Virginia," Katie put in.

"Interesting bit of trivia; where did you come up with that?"

"I studied an almanac in the office."

"Ever the reporter," I told her as we pulled away and began driving toward the heart of the city. "There's the capitol dome," I said. "Looks a lot like the one in Washington."

Within ten minutes, we found the street we were looking for and spotted the address, which turned out to be a three-story brick apartment building that had been built well before the war. I eased up to the curb.

"Time to go in and find out if she's at home. Oh, and here's your prop," Katie said, pulling a Leica camera from her big purse. We stepped into a dark, high-ceilinged lobby that badly needed a fresh coat of paint and some brighter lightbulbs in its dusty ceiling globes.

Carrie Yeager was among more than a dozen tenants listed on a board that had a button next to each name. Katie pushed hers, and after several seconds came a static-filled squawk that sounded like "yes?"

"Miss Yeager, the *Trumpet* back in Ohio is doing a major feature on the life of Logan Mulgrew," Katie spoke into the mouthpiece, "and two of us from the paper are down in the lobby. We would like to get your thoughts on the life of this outstanding citizen."

A long pause. "I'm sorry, but I really don't think I have anything to contribute," came the scratchy reply.

"Oh, I disagree, Miss Yeager. You were privileged to know him well, and everyone else we have talked to was eager to be quoted. It would seem very strange if I had to put in the article that you refused to comment."

Another long silence. "Oh, all right, you can come on up. My number is three-oh-seven."

We rode up in a jerky and shabby automatic elevator that would have terrified Nero Wolfe. In keeping with the overall condition of the building, the third-floor hallway was dimly lit. We peered along its length and saw light coming from the far end, where an apartment door was open. "Down here," a female voice prompted.

That voice belonged, of course, to Carrie Yeager, who turned out to be pretty, and much as Katie had earlier described her: midthirties, close to my height, dark-haired, and the type that people—particularly men—notice. She wore a skirt and sweater and stood in the doorway eyeing us with a wary expression.

"Thank you so much for seeing my photographer and me," Katie said with a smile. "My name is Katie Padgett, and this is Archie." I held up the Leica to verify my role. "May we come in?" she asked.

"Oh yes . . . of course," Carrie said, stepping aside as we entered a small living room with worn furnishings and curtains that looked like they could stand a cleaning.

"I am only in this apartment temporarily," our hostess explained, noticing our dubious looks. "I'll be staying as a caregiver at the home of a man who is getting out of the hospital in the next week or two. His family very kindly put me up here until then. Please sit down."

"Thanks," Katie said, pulling out a reporter's pad and pencil. "Have you done this type of work for a long time?"

"Almost since I got out of school," Carrie replied, "although I was married for two years right after graduation, then got divorced. You don't have to put that in your story, do you?"

"Of course not. The *Trumpet* is mainly interested in the life of Logan Mulgrew, who I am sure you came to know well when you were his wife's caregiver."

Carrie Yeager nodded, lips pursed. "He was a fine gentleman, and he went through a lot because of Mrs. Mulgrew's long illness."

"I'm sure that you must have been a great help to him during that period," Katie prompted.

"I certainly tried to be. Much of the time, his wife was unable to communicate, at least not in what we would term a rational way. I know it was heartbreaking for Log—for Mr. Mulgrew."

"I know that this is a very sensitive question, but do you think the difficulty Mr. Mulgrew had in watching his wife's suffering led to his own death?"

"I . . . suppose that it might have," Carrie said, studying her fingernails. "I have asked myself that many times, of course. I blame myself for not staying in the house after Sylvia—that's Mrs. Mulgrew—died. Maybe I could have prevented what . . . well, what happened."

"Are you convinced that Mr. Mulgrew killed himself?"

"Why . . . of course! What else could it have been?" she asked, eyes wide in an expression of surprise.

"Why did you move out of the Mulgrew house?" Katie asked.

The woman paused several seconds before responding. "It seemed somehow improper for me to continue to live in the home after Mrs. Mulgrew's death. But in retrospect, I wish I had stayed. The truth is, I simply did not realize the full extent of the emotional shape that Mr. Mulgrew was in."

"But you did remain in town?"

"Yes, really more as a favor to Mr. Mulgrew than any other reason. He had no children or close relatives, and he asked me to help him sort through his wife's clothing and other possessions."

"That must have been hard—for both of you."

"It was, but far more for him than for me. Every time he looked at a dress of hers, he would reminisce about an event where she wore it."

"How would you say that people in town viewed Logan Mulgrew?"

Carrie shook her head. "I really don't know. I never got involved in the business part of his life, and at home, he never talked about the bank or anything else he was involved with in the town."

"Did he have many visitors?"

"Not very often. Oh, a few times one of his assistants from the bank came over with some papers for him to sign. Those were on days that he stayed home from work because the doctor came to examine his wife, and Mr. Mulgrew wanted to be there to talk to him afterward."

"Did you know that Mr. Mulgrew had a gun at home?"

"Yes, I did," Carrie said. "He kept it in a desk drawer in the living room. He showed it to me once early on and said, 'You are here alone with my wife a lot, and this house is fairly isolated. I really believe any kind of break-in is unlikely, but if something were to happen, you need to know how to protect yourself—and the house.'"

"Did he show you how to use the gun?"

"Sort of. He took all the bullets out and had me pull the trigger a couple of times just to get the feel of it, and then he put the bullets back in."

"And you never fired it?"

Carrie laughed nervously. "Of course not. Why would I?"

"No reason, just asking. Do you mind if my photographer takes a couple of pictures of you?"

"I guess not, although it seems like I really don't have much to add to your story about Mr. Mulgrew."

"This will be a major piece about Logan Mulgrew, and we'll need photos of anyone who had a major role in his life."

"I would hardly call mine a major role," Carrie protested, but she did let me take some shots, with her wearing both a smile and a serious expression, as I had suggested.

"One last question, Miss Yeager," Katie said. "How would you describe your relationship to Mr. Mulgrew."

"He was my employer, of course."

"Is that all he was?"

"What do you mean by that?" Carrie demanded, jerking upright and frowning.

"It seemed a natural thing to ask, given how often the two of you were seen together in public."

"I do not like your insinuation, and I would like you both to leave right now!" she said in a quavering voice as she stood. We got up and walked out as the door was slammed behind us.

"Let's look for a spot to grab a late lunch," I said to Katie when we were back in the car. After a two-block drive, we found a restaurant that advertised "Steaks. Chops. Burgers. Voted the Best in Town!"

After we had settled into a booth and ordered—corned beef on rye for me, a ham and cheese sandwich for Katie—I said, "You saved the best for last."

"A good reporter's strategy—ask the toughest question at the end of the interview. If you ask that earlier, you're likely to be tossed out."

"We *were* tossed out."

"But not until after we got a reaction from her. I am absolutely positive she and Mulgrew were having an affair."

"What makes you so sure?"

"I thought she seemed awfully nervous, or maybe *edgy* is a better word."

"Being interviewed for a newspaper article can make a lot of people nervous, even when it's a small paper like the *Trumpet*—no offense meant."

"None taken. Well, maybe you're right. But I still have a feeling that Carrie Yeager is somehow off-center."

"Maybe. Now be honest with me, Katie," I said, leaning forward. "There isn't going to be an article by you about Logan Mulgrew in the *Trumpet*, is there?"

The color rose in her face. "Well . . . probably not *just* about him. But I thought it was important to try to smoke out the Yeager woman. I still feel she had something to do with Mulgrew's death. She may have actually pulled the trigger. After all, she told us that she did know about the gun."

"True. I had to wonder, though, whether she is aware enough about newspaper photographers to realize that most of them use a press camera like a Speed Graphic and not a little Leica."

"Aha, Archie Goodwin. Your big-city bias is showing through. Maybe they use those kinds of cameras on the large dailies like the ones you're familiar with, but here a Leica is common. I've even used that very one to take pictures to go with my articles. We don't have a staff photographer, just a freelancer. All the reporters take their own pictures most of the time. Anything to save our almighty bosses' money."

"Okay, I'll concede you that point. What do you plan to do about Miss Yeager now?"

"I haven't decided yet. And what are you going to do yourself? You told me you've spent time with Charles Purcell and Harold Mapes. What's your opinion of them as prospective killers?"

"To use your own phrase, I haven't decided yet."

"Do you have anyone else in mind?" Katie asked. I told her about my plans to meet with Lester Newman and Eldon Kiefer.

"So it's clear that you don't think that I've already identified the killer," she said, exasperation creeping into her voice.

"I am just keeping an open mind, as Nero Wolfe has taught me to do over the years. Now let's eat. All this talk has made me hungry."

CHAPTER 16

On the drive back to Ohio, we continued to discuss the Mulgrew affair and possible killers of the banker. Our conversation was somewhat strained, however, mainly because Katie seemed miffed that I did not buy into her theory that Carrie Yeager had fired the shot sending Logan Mulgrew to eternity.

"What motive would Miss Yeager have for killing Mulgrew?" I asked.

"As I said before, I think she's more than a little unbalanced."

"She seemed pretty normal to me, albeit somewhat nervous, as we discussed."

"Normal? Maybe it really takes a woman to really read another woman, Archie. For instance, I noticed how she had trouble making eye contact."

"Okay, maybe the lady is a little bit shady, if you'll pardon my rhyming," I said, trying to lighten the mood. When that didn't work, I tried another approach.

"I should think you would be suspicious of Eldon Kiefer, the father of that young woman Mulgrew supposedly impregnated," I told Katie. "After all, when you called him, didn't he tell you to go straight to hell, or words to that effect?"

"Not words to that effect," Katie snapped. "Those were the precise words."

"Well, what about Kiefer then?"

Katie was behaving in a petulant manner, sitting in the passenger seat of the convertible with arms folded firmly across her chest and looking straight ahead as if transfixed by the winding two-lane highway we were rolling over.

When she didn't answer, I persisted. "You mentioned earlier that when Kiefer is home from his trucking trips, he hangs out in a local tavern. Which one?"

"Charlie's Tap, so I hear. I've never been in the place. Do you plan to talk to him in the bar, or at home?"

"I thought the bar might be a better spot, although I might have to go there several times to find him."

"Well, as you know, he can be pretty ornery. And although I've never laid eyes on the man, I've learned that he's something of a fitness buff."

"How old is he?"

"Close to fifty, I think, but he is said to have the build of a much younger man."

"Sounds like you are trying to discourage me."

"I just want you to know what you could be up against," Katie said, arms still folded and face set.

"I appreciate your concern," I said with a grin. "I will watch my step." We didn't do much talking the rest of the way back. It was clear Katie preferred to pout, and I was not one to try talking the woman out of it.

Back at the house after dropping Katie off at her apartment,

I gave my mother a quick rundown of the day's activities. "What surprised you most from your trip?" she asked.

"Katie Padgett's insistence that Carrie was a prime suspect—actually *the* prime suspect—in Mulgrew's murder, if indeed he really was murdered."

"Do you think it was murder, Archie?"

"I'm . . . still not sure. I've gone back and forth on this, and I can't make up my mind. One thing that makes me think it was murder is the shot that got fired into Katie's apartment window. I know I'm no Nero Wolfe by any stretch of the imagination, and it's being proven right here."

"I am just a simple, semirural Ohio woman, but as I have come to understand your working relationship with Nero Wolfe, you go out and round up the suspects and deliver them to Mr. Wolfe, who then proceeds to identify the guilty party, right?"

"Simple, semirural Ohio woman, eh? Hah! You taught English in grade school and high school for heaven knows how long while raising a family. And at the same time, you kept the books for the farm so Dad could concentrate on the livestock and the crops."

"I just did what I had to do."

"You sure did, Mom, and in spades, as they say. As to your observation about how Wolfe and I work together, that pretty well summarizes it. Maybe, just maybe, I can round up all those I feel might have ended Logan Mulgrew's life. But then what?"

"One thing at a time. It seems like you're getting ahead of yourself. Have you talked to everyone you have suspicions about?"

"No, there are those two others I mentioned earlier—Lester Newman and Eldon Kiefer. Both of them had plenty of reason to dislike Mulgrew."

"Oh yes, of course. I remember now. Newman is the brother of Mr. Mulgrew's wife, and you said that Eldon Kiefer's daughter may very well have been assaulted and even impregnated by Logan Mulgrew."

"Now all I have to figure out is how to approach these two guys. But first, I should phone New York to find out how things are doing in my absence. I'll call and reverse the charges."

"You will do no such thing, Archie Goodwin!" my mother said in a scolding tone I recognized from my boyhood. "You are a guest in this house, and you will not be paying for telephone calls from here. Besides, I rarely use long distance. The last time I did was to see how you were doing in your big city. Now you make your call. I'll go upstairs and give you some privacy."

"No need for that, Mom. No secrets will be involved here."

She went upstairs anyway, and I did the long-distance routine with a chirping operator. After two rings, I heard the voice of Saul Panzer, saying "Nero Wolfe's office."

"I must say, you have got a fine telephone voice," I told him.

"But of course I have. How are things down in beautiful Ohio?"

"Just fine. Anything I should know about life on West Thirty-Fifth Street?"

"No new business, if that's what you're wondering. What I can report is that your boss, who is of course upstairs with his orchids right now, is one fine gin rummy player."

"Uh-oh, I forgot to warn you that Wolfe is something of a hustler."

"But I just taught him the game, and he's been winning more often than me. And as you know, I'm no slouch at the game."

"As I long ago learned to my regret. I also learned to my regret never to underestimate Nero Wolfe in games of any kind where cash is on the line.

"Case in point: Years back, we played darts, or 'javelins' as Wolfe called them. We tacked playing cards on a corkboard, and the idea was to get a better poker hand than the other guy by sticking darts into specific cards. In a couple of months, Wolfe milked me for eighty-five bucks. And bear in mind that this was someone who hadn't—at least to my knowledge—ever thrown darts or played poker before and until we played didn't know the difference between a straight and a full house."

"Well, I haven't lost eighty-five yet, but I am definitely behind. You had better come home before he cleans me out. By the way, when *are* you coming back?"

"I'm not sure, but probably fairly soon. Does Wolfe miss me?"

"If so, he hasn't mentioned it. I hope you're not getting into trouble down there."

"No more than usual. Is my boss keeping you busy?"

"Not overly. I usually only come in mornings, to sort his mail, pay a few bills, that sort of thing. Today I'm working later because Wolfe gave me some dictation and I'm typing up a stack of letters. And for the record, I think Fritz misses you."

"Speaking of Fritz, I hope you're taking advantage of his culinary skills."

"That's the best part of the job, Archie. I stay for lunch every day before heading off to take care of my own work. But tonight, I'm going to be here for dinner as well. We're having squabs with sausage and sauerkraut. Eat your heart out thinking about it."

"Glad to know you still have some clients, Saul," I said, ignoring his last comment. "You'll need the cash infusion to cover your gin rummy losses if you persist in going up against Nero Wolfe, that well-known card sharp."

"Thanks for the advice. I'll keep that in mind. Tell your mother I said hello. A fine lady."

"She has asked after you as well. She thinks you're an all-right guy, which just goes to show how good you are at fooling people."

"I'd love to stay on the line and keep bantering with you, as pleasant as this has been, but I have work to do for Mr. Wolfe, unless you've got something else that you want to say."

"Nothing that could be printed in a family newspaper," I told him, and we rang off.

CHAPTER 17

My sparring with Saul was therapeutic, and when our call ended, I sat for several minutes in the living room collecting my thoughts. I opted to tackle Lester Newman first, thereby getting the drive down to Waverly out of the way.

At that moment, my mother came downstairs. "Is everything in New York all right?" she asked.

"Maybe too good. They don't seem to miss me. I've decided my next step is to go to Waverly and see Lester Newman. That is, if I can find him."

"Waverly is in our phone directory, Archie. Maybe he's listed. So you've decided to push ahead?"

"I have."

"You were always our most headstrong one growing up, and you still are. You remind me so much of your father—even more so as you get older."

"Is that a compliment?"

"Definitely. You both always knew what you wanted, and by heaven, you were going to get it."

"Maybe that's why he and I didn't always get along. We were too much alike."

Sure enough, Lester Newman was listed in the regional phone book Mom had, along with his address in Waverly, which I vaguely remember as being a quiet little burg.

The next morning, after a drive of less than a half hour, I found myself in Waverly, which still seemed like a quiet little burg, small enough that I quickly found the street where Newman lived. I also found his house, a modest two-story white stucco number that would soon need a paint job.

I walked up an uneven sidewalk with grass growing up through the cracks and pressed the bell. After a wait of close to a minute, the front door opened slightly, and a hunched-over man with a gray crew cut glanced up at me through one eye, the other one being closed. "What do you want?" he rasped. "I'm not buying whatever it is that you're selling."

"And I'm not selling anything. My name is Archie Goodwin, and I would like to talk to you about your late sister, Sylvia Mulgrew."

"And just why would I want to talk to *you*, Mr. . . . . Goodwin?" Newman asked through the narrow slit. "By the way, just who are you?"

"I am a private detective, and I happen to be interested in the lives of your late sister and her husband. It has been said that your sister may not have died from natural causes."

"That so? And just where has that been said?"

At least I had piqued his interest. "Up where she and her husband had lived," I answered.

Slowly, the door swung farther open, revealing that Newman was supporting himself with a cane. "All right, come on inside," he said in a grumpy tone. I found myself in a small but neat living room.

"Have a seat," he muttered, gesturing toward a sofa. "You caught me as I was just finishing up washing the dishes, but that can wait."

I looked around the room I was in and focused on a framed display on the far wall. Against a blue velvet background was mounted an array of army medals and ribbons, which I recognized.

I pointed at the display. "That is very impressive, sir," I told him. "Good Conduct Medal, World War II Victory Medal, Purple Heart, and best of all, the Distinguished Service Cross, along with a lot of ribbons."

"I earned every dang one of 'em," he said gruffly. "I also should have gotten the Medal of Honor, too, but those bastards . . . oh, never mind. Say, you seem to know your medals. Were you in?"

"Yes, but not like you. I was stuck in Washington the whole time."

"As an officer, I suppose?"

"Yes, major."

"Hell, I should be calling you *sir*, not the other way around. But that's okay, everybody did their part. I was a platoon sergeant, Fifth Army, at Anzio."

"One of the bloodiest battles of the war, so I read and heard," I remarked.

"I'm here to tell ya. It's the closest thing to hell that I'll ever see before I kick the bucket. And it's what made me the wreck I am now. Say, you got me talking about the damned war, and

I still don't know why you are so interested in my poor dead sister. Tell me more."

Time to come clean. "As I told you, I am a private detective, based in New York, although I'm originally from these parts and am currently staying with my mother just a few miles north of here."

"Goodwin . . . Goodwin. Say, wasn't there a farmer by that name up on the Portsmouth Road at one time?" Newman asked.

"My father, dead for a number of years now."

"Back to my question: Why all the interest in Sylvia?"

"I'm curious about the circumstances of her death, and the death of her husband."

My host narrowed his good eye in my direction. "I'm curious, too, very curious," Newman said, spacing the words for emphasis. "First off, let me tell you that I'm a lot younger than I look, even though I still had to talk the army into letting me enlist because I was over the stupid age limit that they had set. The war added a lot of years to me, not that I'm complaining, mind you."

"So noted."

"Even though we were brother and sister, Sylvia was a lot older, and she was almost like a mother to me. In fact, my late wife used to say, 'It's almost as if you had two mothers when you were growing up.' And she was right about that. Sylvia looked after me when I was a kid, and I can tell you that I was a terror."

"Then at some point your sister married Logan Mulgrew," I said.

"That miserable son of a bitch. I knew from the start that the man was a rotter, but Sylvia couldn't, or wouldn't, see it. Mulgrew could be charming, no question, but it was easy for me to see right through him. Even down here in Waverly, the word was getting through about Mulgrew and his . . . his *escapades*."

"Did you ever mention anything to your sister about all this?"

"I started to once, years ago, but she cut me off in midsentence. She said something like 'There is too much idle gossip going around our town, and I refuse to listen to it.' She even quoted from the book of James in the New Testament about the tongue being 'a world of evil among the parts of the body.'"

"Well, when people begin using the Bible in an argument, you know their position is pretty well set," I told him.

"Yeah, I knew there was really no use of my going on. Sylvia wasn't about to listen. And then when she started getting sick, Mulgrew wouldn't even let me see her. He said I upset her too much, which was total hogwash."

"Do you have any thoughts about your sister's death—and Mulgrew's?"

"Before we go any further, Mr. Goodwin, has someone hired you to poke into all this?"

"Believe it or not, I haven't been hired by anybody. But there are people who seem to think your sister may not have died of natural causes, and that her husband may not have killed himself. Because I happened to be in town visiting my mother, some of these people have asked me to look into it. That's mainly the truth," I told him, spreading my hands in what I hoped would be seen as a gesture of candor.

Newman peered at me for several seconds before speaking. "You were an officer, a major, no less, and I respect you for that, even though I had to answer to some second looeys who didn't know their heads from their tails. You know, a lotta people around here think that I'm tetched in my attic," he said, tapping his forehead with a gnarled index finger. "And I suppose maybe I am at that. I don't always feel right, and I don't always remember things that I should. And sometimes I get these headaches like you wouldn't believe. Doc tells me it's because of what I went through in the war, and I'm not about to dispute him in his opinion.

"Now as far as what happened to my sister, I'd hafta say that miserable husband of hers didn't do her any favors."

"What do you mean by that, Mr. Newman?"

"By that I mean she didn't get the kind of medical care she needed, 'specially when her mind began to desert her."

"She had a full-time caregiver, didn't she?"

Newman snorted. "If that's what you want to call that Carrie Yeager floozy her husband brought in to look after Sylvia."

"You don't believe the Yeager woman was qualified?"

Another snort. "Qualified as what—a gold digger? You had better believe that word got down here to me about how friendly Mulgrew and that Yeager woman had become. You know, Mr. Goodwin, I'm something of a loner, don't have a lot of friends, which is just fine by me.

"But some people around this town just can't wait to bring you bad news. There's a woman just across the street here who telephoned me to say she had seen my brother-in-law and that so-called caregiver having what she called 'a cozy dinner' at a restaurant in your town up north while Sylvia was at home and probably alone and suffering."

"What do you think Miss Yeager expected to gain from her friendship with Logan Mulgrew?"

Newman gave me an *Are you an idiot?* look. "Well, what do you think? Money, of course! I can't believe a young woman like her would have any kind of romantic interest in that dried-up old coot."

"Did he leave her anything in his will?" I asked, knowing the answer.

"Not that I've heard. So whatever she was up to apparently didn't work."

"What has become of her?"

"That I couldn't say. And to be honest, I really don't give a tinker's damn."

"That's understandable. Do you think Mrs. Mulgrew was killed?"

Newman paused for several seconds and ran a hand across his brow before answering. "I have asked myself that many times, and I just don't know. I wasn't around, of course; as I told you, I was not welcome. Which means I have no idea the kind of treatment that Sylvia was getting—or not getting. But let's just say that I have my suspicions, strong suspicions."

"Now on to her husband. Do you think that he killed himself?"

The prematurely aged soldier jerked upright and squared his shoulders. "Why are you asking me?"

I flipped a palm. "You knew all the people involved, and I figure you might have some observations, that's all."

"Do I think Mulgrew shot himself because he was devastated over Sylvia's death?"

"Or do you think Mulgrew shot himself at all?"

It was obvious that Newman was getting agitated by the direction in which I was steering the conversation. He began hyperventilating, to the point where I felt he might be having some sort of attack or seizure. I waited as he slowly settled down and his breath became more normal.

He blinked at me as though seeing me for the first time. "I . . . sorry, I . .." He held his head in his hands and shook it vigorously as if to clear it.

"Are you all right, Mr. Newman?"

"I think so, and I need to . . . need to go up to my room and lie down now." He got to his feet slowly and walked toward the stairway to the second floor.

"Can I give you a hand?" I asked.

Newman shook his head but didn't answer and slowly began climbing the steps as he gripped the railing. I went up behind him in case he fell, which seemed like a strong possibility. But he made it to the top and headed for the door to what I assumed was his bedroom. I saw no reason to stay any longer.

CHAPTER 18

I had plenty to think about on the drive back to my mother's house. There was no question that Newman had become psychologically scarred by his war experiences. But did he use that scarring as a figurative crutch to avoid facing an unpleasant reality, one in which he was the shooter of Logan Mulgrew?

He seemed relatively lucid until I started talking about the possibility that Mulgrew might have been killed. Then he became unhinged—or did he? Nero Wolfe has on more than one occasion discussed the ways in which people can use their supposed mental or psychological deficiencies to their benefit by appearing to be more disturbed than they really are. I may have just witnessed such behavior from Lester Newman.

In fact, my boss had been on my mind often since my arrival in Ohio. As I continued to gather information about the deaths of both Logan Mulgrew and his wife, I found myself wondering: *What would Nero Wolfe do with this fact or that comment?* Over the years, I have tried to train myself to think like him, but it has almost never worked. He was born a genius, and I was born . . . well, *not* a genius.

Wolfe may have put it best when I told him once that I had some ideas about a case on which we were working. His response: "Your head full of ideas? Even my death by violence is not too high a price for so rare and happy a phenomenon as that." I should have been insulted, but I wasn't. He was right, and I have long since become aware that my role in our operation is not as a thinker but as a man of action.

That being the case, what action should I now take? First, I had one more individual to meet with—Eldon Kiefer. I was thinking about how best to approach him when I realized I had arrived at my mother's home.

She had seen me coming and held open the front door. "Successful trip?" she asked.

"Mixed. Mr. Newman seems to be a very troubled man."

"Well, the war did a lot of horrible things to a lot of people. I was proud of the fact that you were in the army but was also glad you were stationed in the States."

"And ironically, I wished I had seen combat. Anything going on here?"

"Oh yes. Katie, the intrepid reporter, called—twice. She seemed very curious as to where you were."

"You didn't tell her?"

"Of course not, Archie. I just said you had gone out and were probably visiting some of your old haunts on your first visit back here in a long time."

"You are a good liar, Mom."

"I was not *lying*, I just wasn't being specific."

"Did Katie say why she was looking for me?"

"No, but if I were to make a guess, she was suspicious that you were doing some investigating and leaving her out of it."

"A good guess. Not to take anything away from Katie, but I tend to operate more efficiently when I work alone. What's different here is that after I've collected whatever information I get, there's no Nero Wolfe to unload it on. I've gotten so used to having him do all the thinking that I may have forgotten how to do it myself."

"I don't believe that for a second!" my mother said in an admonishing tone. "I think you are selling yourself short."

"Maybe, but after talking to all these people—and I still have Kiefer left—I'm no closer to figuring things out than when I started."

"Don't you suppose it's possible that Sylvia Mulgrew died of natural causes and her husband really did shoot himself?"

"Yes, it's possible, but I don't believe it, at least in the case of Logan Mulgrew. So far, nothing I've learned about the man would indicate he was so heartbroken over his wife's death that he would kill himself."

"I wish I could be of some help to you, Archie. Unfortunately, as I've told you, I'm not really tuned in to the talk that goes on around town. Sorry."

"Nothing to be sorry about. You are not a gossip, and I happen to like that. It's very possible that I'll go back to New York without having accomplished a darn thing here."

"You've already accomplished something just by being here so that we could have some time together, one-on-one."

"Yeah, that has been nice, no question. But just because we have gotten caught up these last few days is no reason that you shouldn't come to Manhattan in the fall, just as we had planned. Remember, Lily Rowan likes to have somebody to go shopping with at all those pricey clothing and shoe stores."

"As I've mentioned to you before, she hardly needs an excuse," my mother said, rolling her eyes.

"Still, I gather it's more fun to have a partner in crime when shopping," I replied.

"Leave it to my detective son to equate everything to crime. On that subject, when do you plan to see Mr. Kiefer?"

"Possibly as early as tonight, if he happens to be in town and at his favorite watering hole."

CHAPTER 19

After two helpings of my mother's roast chicken, I paged through the telephone directory and found Charlie's Tap, the place Katie Padgett had told me was Eldon Kiefer's hangout. I was on my way.

Charlie's turned out to be a typical—if there is such a thing—neighborhood drinking spot: neon signs in the front window advertising beer brands; polished ebony bar running the length of the room that was longer than wide; half a dozen tables; tiny dance floor, currently unused; and a jukebox that was playing a Johnny Mathis ballad as I stepped in. A couple of heads turned my way and then returned to their drinks. Less than half the stools were occupied. I took a spot at one end of the bar and ordered a draft beer. The bartender, a glum, tight-lipped sort with droopy eyes, slid the foamy stein to a halt in front of me without spilling a drop.

"Is there a guy in here named Kiefer, by chance?" I asked.

"Eldon? Yeah, that's him down there," the barkeep said, indicating a burly man with a crew cut and a scowl. I picked up my beer and walked to an empty stool next to him. "Nice evening, huh?" I said, my version of snappy repertoire.

He grunted something unintelligible. "It's a long time now since I've been back here, in what passes for my hometown," I told him. "Seems like it's about the same as I remember."

He shrugged broad shoulders and drank his beer. "Things don't ever change much around here."

"I suppose not. Since I've been back, all the talk I've been hearing is about that Mulgrew banker shooting himself. Damnedest thing, eh?"

Kiefer didn't respond, so I pushed on. "What do you think would drive a successful old fellow like that to kill himself? Maybe bad health, eh?"

"You tell me," he mumbled, obviously not interested in conversation.

"Quite a puzzler," I pushed on. "Did you know him?"

He glared at me. "Yeah, I knew him, as much as I wanted to."

"I've heard rumors about Mulgrew, and not very nice ones. It seems that he was, well . . ." I let it trail off.

"Well, what?" Kiefer barked, turning to me with a fierce expression. I had awakened him.

"It seems he had a habit of taking advantage of young women, or so I have been told."

"Is that any of your business?" he growled, causing others to look in our direction.

"I'm just commenting on what I've been hearing."

"Well, keep your goddamn commenting to yourself!"

"Sorry," I said, holding up a hand. "I didn't mean to get you all riled up."

"I will show you just who's riled up," Kiefer said, giving me a hard shove that knocked me off my stool and onto the floor on my rear end. As I got to my feet, he reared back and delivered a roundhouse punch in the direction of my jaw that I saw coming. It turned out to be a glancing blow as I backed away, and I delivered a right hand to his chest, which seemed to be made of armor.

Kiefer threw a second punch, which caught me in the shoulder and spun me around. I squared up and aimed a left jab at his face, staggering him. A second left to his gut, which wasn't made of armor, doubled him over and sent him to the floor with a retch. During our flurry, the others along the bar had backed away and the bartender, as I was to learn, got on the telephone to the police.

It seemed like only seconds had passed, although it must have been longer, before a pair of young officers in uniform, one tall and skinny and the other short and well-fed, walked in, tensed and with hands hovering above their holsters. "Okay, what's going on here?" the taller one demanded of the barkeep.

"These two," he said, pointing at Kiefer and me, "they started mixing it up. They went at it before I even knew what was going on."

"All right, you brawlers, get over there against the wall. Hey, wait a minute, it's you again," Shorty snapped, aiming his comment at Kiefer. "This is the third or fourth time you've gotten into a scrape with somebody. You need to control your—"

"It's the first time anything's ever happened with Eldon in *my* place, Officer," the bartender interrupted. "There hasn't been any trouble in here in years. You can check your records."

"Yeah, Eldon's always pretty quiet when he's here," one of the regulars put in. "Maybe it's this other guy that caused the trouble," he said, pointing at me.

"You, I'm sorry to say, I know," the chubby cop told Kiefer and then turned to me. "You, I don't know. Let's see some identification." I handed him my wallet.

"Goodwin, eh? Related to the Mrs. Goodwin who lives out on the Portsmouth Road?"

"My mother. I'm in town visiting her."

"You're in town stirring up trouble, is more like it," he said with a sneer. "Hold on—you are a private cop?" He fingered my license and looked at me to see if my face matched the photo.

"In New York."

"Maybe brawling is common where you come from, Mr. Goodwin, but we don't take kindly to it here in what you probably think of as the sticks."

"For the record, if anybody's keeping score, I did not throw the first punch."

"He's right," another of the onlookers said. "I saw Eldon shove him off his barstool and onto the floor. It was the start."

"What do you have to say to that?" the beanpole asked Kiefer, who was wiping blood off his nose.

"I got nothin' to say."

The officer turned to me. "Okay, let's hear your story. What did you tell Kiefer that got him all worked up?"

"I just started talking about some of what's been going on around town."

"Do you know Kiefer?"

"No, I just happened to sit down next to him."

"That's not true, Officer," the bartender said. "When this man—Goodwin, isn't it?—came in, he asked if Eldon was here, and I pointed him out."

"Had Mr. Goodwin ever been in here before?"

"Not to my knowledge, and I'm behind the bar ninety-five percent of the time we're open. Now I happen to run a peaceful place, and—"

"Yeah, yeah, I know, I know, you made your point before, don't push it," the tall cop said. "Mr. Goodwin, why did you specifically seek out Eldon Kiefer?"

"I'd heard, I can't remember where, that he knows a lot about what goes on around here."

"And just why are you interested in 'what goes on around here'? Does it have something to do with you being a private detective?"

"I'd prefer not to say any more here."

"Kiefer doesn't want to talk, and you don't want to talk. Well, that's just fine, because we're going to be taking you both down to the station to meet Chief Blankenship. Maybe he can loosen up your tongues."

CHAPTER 20

The police allowed both Kiefer and me to drive our own vehicles to the police headquarters, although we had to follow close behind their patrol car with its flashing lights, which made for a poor man's parade through the downtown streets, drawing curious looks from pedestrians.

Our motley little entourage pulled up in front of the police station, an unimpressive one-story brick structure that I recognized from my youth, although I never had occasion to be inside. We trooped in, Kiefer in the lead, followed by me and then Mutt and Jeff, the unmatched pair of young coppers. They never drew their weapons, apparently seeing the two of us as harmless.

Hardly surprising, Kiefer and I did not speak to each other. He held a handkerchief to the nose I had bloodied, and I felt a sharp pain in my shoulder where his right had landed.

I regretted, at least slightly, having baited Kiefer back in the bar, but then, I didn't expect the violent reaction that resulted, although maybe I should have, given what Katie Padgett had told me about him and his volatility. It seemed the man was like a grenade ready to discharge.

"We've got a couple of would-be prizefighters here," the tall cop said to the bald desk sergeant, who wore a bored expression. "My guess is that the chief would like to meet them."

"I'll tell him you're here," the sarge said with a world-weary sigh, picking up a phone and muttering something into the mouthpiece. He hung up and said, "Okay, go on back and see him."

Blankenship's quarters were about what I would have expected of a small-town top cop's office: bare walls; a single window looking out onto a parking lot; a three-drawer gunmetal filing cabinet; a neat maple desk with a framed color photograph of his wife and two young children; and a plaque that read *Chief Thomas Robert Blankenship.*

The chief had his head down as he signed a small stack of papers. Finishing the last one, he looked up grim-faced, first at me and then at Kiefer, shaking his head.

"I recognize them both, for different reasons," he said to his cops. "This one"—he indicated Kiefer—"has been here on at least a couple occasions. He can't seem to control his temper. You boys have brought him in before, the last time was after he got into a fistfight with the driver of a grocery truck just off the courthouse square. It was when—"

"I got cut off!" Kiefer yelped. "That idiot almost rammed me!"

"Mr. Kiefer," Blankenship said in a patient tone, steepling his hands, "if that had been the only incident you were involved in, I wouldn't be terribly concerned. But a pattern seems to have emerged here. Is there anything you care to tell us about what happened in that bar tonight?"

"This guy"—Kiefer gestured at me with a thumb—"kept jabbering to me. He wouldn't shut up."

"Did he threaten you?"

"Uh . . . well, not in so many words."

"Tell me what 'not in so many words' means," Blankenship said, still in his father-confessor mode.

Kiefer shifted from one leg to the other, still dabbing at his bloodied nose. "Well, he wanted to talk about Logan Mulgrew's death."

"Did he now? Any idea why he happened to pick you to discuss that subject with?"

"No, not really."

"Had you ever met this man before?" the chief asked, gesturing at me.

"Never, not once."

"Did you know Logan Mulgrew?"

"I had met him."

"What was your opinion of the man?"

"I didn't like him," Kiefer said with a snarl.

"Any particular reason why that is?"

"My daughter worked for him at the bank at one time, and he, well . . . he wasn't very nice to her." I could tell Kiefer was working to rein in that volatile temper.

"Do you mean that he was abusive?" Blankenship asked.

"I don't want to say any more." Kiefer folded beefy arms across his chest and stuck out his chin.

The chief leaned back in his chair and sighed, clasping his hands behind his head. "So let me see if I can get this straight: This gentleman here, who you claim that you never met, began talking to you about Logan Mulgrew, and you got irritated and started a fight with him. Do I have an accurate version of events?"

"Uh . . . pretty much," Kiefer said. I could tell he wanted to sit down even more than I did, but Blankenship's method was to keep both of us on our feet.

"Do you have anything else to say?"

My erstwhile sparring partner looked down at the floor and shook his head. "No, nothin'," he mumbled.

"You have caused trouble on several occasions in the past, Mr. Kiefer, and each time you have received only a warning," Blankenship said. "And I am going to give you this one final warning, sir: the next time you find yourself in this building because of your actions, you will be slapped with a fine or jail time—or both. Have I made myself clear to you?" Kiefer said nothing.

"Is that *clear*, Mr. Kiefer?"

"Yes, sir."

"Good, now get out of here, and heaven help you if I see you in my office again!"

As Kiefer shuffled out and shut the door behind him, Blankenship turned to me. "Somehow, I knew I would be meeting you again, Mr. Goodwin. Are you one of those people trouble follows?"

"I wouldn't say so," I said, gripping my throbbing shoulder.

The chief leaned forward in his chair and considered me. "You believe Logan Mulgrew was murdered, don't you?"

"His death seems suspicious," I stated, easing into the guest chair in front of the chief's desk without being asked. He did not object.

"I am afraid that on this subject, we must agree to disagree, Mr. Goodwin. But being open-minded, I would like to hear your reasons for believing Mulgrew's death was a murder."

"I did not say that he definitely was murdered, I said his death was suspicious—in fact, *very* suspicious."

"Tell me just what makes this death so suspicious, Mr. Goodwin."

"Of course, I never met Mulgrew, but it didn't take me long to learn that he was an extremely disliked man. He made numerous enemies in this corner of the state. His calculated rumormongering caused one man's bank to collapse almost before it got started and ruined his life in the process. He foreclosed on a farmer and also all but ruined his life and his livelihood. He is said to have abused another man's daughter and possibly gotten her pregnant. He openly carried on a relationship with his wife's caregiver as she, his wife, lay dying. How's that for starters?"

"You are a private detective of some note, sir. Do you have a client in the Mulgrew affair?"

"I do not."

"So should I assume that you have become interested in Mr. Mulgrew's death as a simple matter of professional curiosity? That would seem to be most high-minded and noble of you."

"Don't try to make me out to be something I'm not," I told him. "But when I smell a rat, there is usually a rat in the area. I should also add to my narrative that those people I mentioned who have reason to dislike Logan Mulgrew also had openly expressed their anger toward him before his death."

"For someone so recently arrived here, you seem to have amassed an impressive storehouse of information about our community," the chief observed dryly. "Would one of your sources just happen to be a young woman journalist?"

"I have talked to several people about the Mulgrew death."

"A diplomatic answer. You mentioned earlier the abuse of one man's daughter and her possible pregnancy. Would that man be Eldon Kiefer?"

"It would."

"Which would at least begin to explain why you were in Charlie's Tap tonight. Do you suspect him of Mr. Mulgrew's murder?"

"He certainly is one of the people who had reason to dislike Logan Mulgrew. Make that people who had reason to *intensely* dislike the man."

"All right, I will not dispute the fact that Mulgrew was not popular with a number of folks," Blankenship said. "That's on one side of the ledger. On the other side, which I happen to subscribe to, is that the man was mourning the loss of his wife of decades, which understandably could lead to a suicide."

"However, in the months following Mrs. Mulgrew's death, her husband hardly behaved like someone in mourning," I countered. "From what I have been able to ascertain, he showed no signs whatever of depression, rather the contrary."

"I consider that to be circumstantial evidence of his moods," the chief said.

"Perhaps. What are your thoughts about the gunshot fired into the apartment of Miss Padgett?"

"As I have previously stated, I believe it to be the work of someone who had been overserved and unfortunately chose to let off steam with a firearm. For the record, although it is hardly any of your business, we dug that shell from the wall of Miss Padgett's apartment, and it did not match the caliber of the bullet that killed Logan Mulgrew. I believe I told you this already as well."

"Well, I also ask you again, is it usual for gunshots to be discharged in the middle of town?"

The chief shifted in his chair. "You keep harping on this. It's the first time it's happened since I have been in this office. But I still believe it to be a coincidence. Mr. Goodwin, I will be candid. Your meddling is not welcome here. Although I do not know your mother well, I happen to have great respect for her based on our limited contact with each other. I would hate to have her embarrassed by your behavior."

"Is that a threat?"

"I prefer to think of it as a warning."

"Consider, then, that I have been warned."

"Your attitude does not comfort me, Mr. Goodwin."

"I am sorry to hear that. Do you plan to charge me?"

"Not at the moment. I believe Mr. Kiefer must bear the brunt of your contretemps with him."

"You certainly know how to use the language, Chief."

"It may surprise you to learn that I am a college graduate. Not all policemen are like the ones you probably are used to in New York."

"Big-city cops happen to come in all shapes, sizes, and levels of education and intelligence. I try never to place people in boxes."

"That is good to know. What do you plan to do now, Mr. Goodwin?"

"In what way?"

"What I mean is, are you intent upon continuing this investigation of Logan Mulgrew's death?"

"I have yet to be persuaded that the man was not murdered."

Blankenship pressed his palms over his eyes, perhaps wishing that when he opened them I would be gone. "If I find that you are in any way impeding the work of the department, I will take action. So far, I have avoided a confrontation, in part because of my respect for your mother. But I warn you that I will not hesitate to take you into custody if I find that you've become a public nuisance."

"Public nuisance? Just what does that charge entail?"

"That is left to my discretion, as well as to the discretion of the local justice of the peace."

"Am I free to leave?"

"No one is stopping you," Blankenship said with a grim expression. "But I repeat my warning, Mr. Goodwin. You are very close to wearing out your welcome in this community, at least in the eyes of the police department. I have no personal animosity toward you, but I really hope we do not have occasion to meet again."

CHAPTER 21

I walked out of the police station that balmy June evening wondering why I was staying in town. There was my mother, of course, but the chances were strong that I would be seeing her in New York in the autumn. It was true I was suspicious—damned suspicious—of how Logan Mulgrew met his end, but so what?

Other than Katie Padgett and Aunt Edna, nobody I was aware of seemed to care why and how Mulgrew died. As I told Blankenship, I had no client, so there was no money to be made in the pursuit of what could be termed a pointless exercise. And I risked causing my mother embarrassment by hanging around and upsetting not only the local constabulary but others in the community as well, some of whom surely resented the presence of a "city slicker" in their midst.

When I got back to the house, my mother greeted me as I walked into the living room. "You have been gone a long time, not that it is any of my business. Is everything all right?"

"It has been suggested by Chief Tom Blankenship that I have worn out my welcome here," I said, dropping into a wing chair and rubbing my sore shoulder. "And I believe that the man may be right."

"Well, you certainly haven't worn it out as far as I am concerned!" she told me. "Is the chief upset because you have continued looking into Mr. Mulgrew's death?"

"He is indeed. And I'm beginning to wonder why I am spending so much time on all this."

"Well, while you continue your wondering, I should mention that you have had two telephone calls: Miss Padgett, or Katie, as you now refer to her, phoned, wondering why she hasn't heard from you and asked that you call her; and your aunt Edna, which shouldn't surprise you. She tried to make it sound like she was inquiring as to my health, but my dear sister is really quite transparent. After I assured her that I was just fine, thank you, she said: 'Should I assume that Archie is still staying with you?'

"I told her you were and asked if she would like you to telephone her. The response: 'Oh yes, that would be very nice. I do like talking to him.'"

"I'm afraid my presence here has turned you into an unpaid answering service, and I'm sorry."

She waved my comment away. "Don't worry yourself one bit. I am rather enjoying the intrigue, if that is what you call it."

"That's as good a word as any," I said. "I suppose I should get in touch with these two ladies."

"I will leave you to make your calls in private," my mother said.

"Not necessary," I answered, but she went upstairs anyway, and I telephoned Katie Padgett.

"Archie! I wondered why I haven't heard from you. Is everything all right?"

"Yes, it is."

"Have you found out anything new about . . . you know?"

"No, I find myself pretty much at a dead end."

"Well, I have some wonderful news—at least I'm sure you will think it's wonderful. The *Trumpet* has a new managing editor, Martin Chase, who wants to shake things up. He's under thirty, and he comes from a little paper in Kentucky; and though the *Trumpet* isn't all that big itself, the move is a step up for him. He wants to win a Pulitzer here. 'Small papers from places like Lost Gulch, Arizona, really do win them sometimes,' he says."

"Sounds like a man who has got big plans."

"I'll say, and just listen to this: I've pitched him the idea that I do a long feature, or maybe even a series of pieces, called 'The Mystery of Logan Mulgrew's Death,' in which I talk about all the people who could have wanted him dead. And he likes the idea!"

"Interesting, but don't you—and the *Trumpet*—risk running into legal problems by bringing in all these names as potential suspects?"

"Martin says it's all in how we handle it. That doesn't trouble him in the least. I'm going to start writing today. I'm really excited."

"Do you still think Carrie Yeager is guilty?"

"Absolutely, Archie."

"Will your writing reflect that?"

"That is an excellent question. I told Martin about her, and he feels we should present all the suspects—and you know who they are—equally, to heighten the mystery."

"This man sounds like he should be working for one of New York's tabloid dailies."

"I wouldn't be surprised to learn that's his ultimate goal," Katie said. "By the way, one of my first calls on this assignment for Martin was to Donna Newman, who believes as I do that Carrie killed Mulgrew. She wanted me to tell you that she's sorry she called Chief Blankenship to complain about you. She said she overreacted to your questions. Did the chief ever talk to you about that?"

"He did. In fact, we have talked again since my visit to her."

"Really? Anything I should know about?" Katie asked in an excited tone.

"I don't think so. Chief Blankenship would be happy if I went back to New York, though."

"Are you planning to go?" This time, I couldn't tell if her tone was excitement, disappointment, or something in between.

"I haven't made up my mind yet; I will let you know."

"Please do, Archie. I would miss you. But I have to go now, I have lots to do."

Next, I put in a call to Aunt Edna. "Archie, I've been wondering what you've been up to. I have something to tell you."

"I am all ears, as they say."

She cleared her throat, perhaps as a preamble to news. "It seems there's a growing feeling around town that Carrie Yeager killed Logan Mulgrew."

"Really? How have you happened to pick up this information?"

Another throat clearing. "I heard it from three different people at my bridge club yesterday, and this morning when I was at the dry cleaners, Mrs. Zeller told me she had been told by her dentist that the police could be charging the Yeager woman any time. It seems they've learned that she is living in Charleston, West Virginia."

"Most interesting. Any idea what the source of these rumors is?"

"No, and I'm not sure that I would call them rumors, Archie. The talk appears to be so widespread that I have to wonder if the net isn't closing in on Miss Yeager."

"Have you talked to our favorite reporter about all this?" I asked.

"Oh yes. Miss Padgett says she has heard the same things, and from a number of sources. The story going around is that Carrie Yeager thought she would develop a permanent relationship with Mr. Mulgrew, and that he apparently discouraged such a relationship."

"Do you believe that?"

"Well, it certainly sounds feasible. Logan Mulgrew was notorious for his fickle nature when it came to women."

"Yet his wife stayed married to him for all those years."

"She did, probably because she really had no other options," Aunt Edna said firmly. "They never had children, so she did not have anybody else to run off to live with. And after all, whatever else Mulgrew was, he was a good provider of material things, and Sylvia is said to have lived well in that big old pile of brick and stone, at least until her health deserted her."

"Do you have any idea whether Chief Blankenship has shown any interest in the case?"

"I don't, although I can tell you this: Miss Padgett has confidentially told me—and I know I can trust you with this—that the *Trumpet* is planning a major story that may shed light on what *really* happened. It seems the paper has a new young editor who is not afraid of stirring things up."

"That is very interesting, Aunt Edna. Do you care to make a prediction as to how all this will play out?"

"Oh dear, making predictions is hardly a specialty of mine, but since you asked, I have to wonder about Carrie Yeager, although I'm not ready to say she killed Logan Mulgrew. Right now, I'm really looking forward to the *Trumpet* story."

"Has Miss Padgett told you whether she's going to talk to the police chief for her story? It seems to me she can't do this article without quoting him."

"Archie, I do admit that I was curious about that very thing, but I didn't ask her. I did not want to appear to be nosy." Aunt Edna not wanting to appear nosy? That will be the day, I thought as I called to my mother, who was still upstairs. I craved another piece of that apple pie we had for dessert, and I thought she might want to join me. She did.

CHAPTER 22

Finding out that Katie Padgett was working on what sounded like an exposé of the Logan Mulgrew death—and maybe that of his wife, as well—made me decide to postpone my return to New York for a while. Things could get interesting in the old hometown.

As I paged through the *Trumpet* the next morning at breakfast, I saw an item in the "Around the State" feature that would give me at least one good reason to hang around a little longer. "Look at this, Mom," I said, handing her the paper. "There's a big quilt exhibition that's just opened at the state fairgrounds in Columbus."

"That's very nice, dear," my mother said as she blew on the coffee in her cup to cool it. "Since when have you been interested in quilts?"

"Well, you're interested in them, and you have got a bunch of county fair ribbons to prove it. What do you say that we drive up to Columbus?"

"Really, Archie, you shouldn't feel that you have to indulge me."

"I would be indulging myself, too," I told her. "You know how much I like to drive, and this is a perfect day to head north with the top down on that convertible of mine that's parked out behind the house, just waiting to be turned loose on the beckoning highways and byways of the Buckeye State."

"My goodness, you sound almost poetic. Who would have ever thought that, given your English grades in high school?"

"Hey, remember that I once got an A-plus on a paper I wrote about all the presidents who came from Ohio. Have you forgotten?"

She laughed. "How could I? For weeks afterward, you kept reminding your father and me about it. Actually, for all the complaining you did about school, you really were a pretty decent student."

"I did complain a lot, though, didn't I? And then later, it didn't take me long to realize that college was a waste of time for me. What do you say we take off for Columbus?"

"How can I say no to such an offer? I just hope you don't get bored looking at a lot of quilts."

"I'll take my chances. Let's go!"

Less than a half hour later, we were on the road north, my mother wearing a scarf on her head.

"The last time I rode in a car with a top down was your father's old jalopy," she said. "I'm sure you must remember it?"

"Of course I do. It had more rattles than a nursery school. I figured it was always about to fall apart. I never knew why he held on to the damn thing for so long."

"Remember, he had a perfectly good pickup truck, too. He kept the jalopy because he loved to occasionally take a spin without a roof over his head. Like father, like son."

"I guess you're right. Nero Wolfe never saw a need for us to have a convertible, but I argued so much that he finally gave in. He won't ride in it, of course. I have enough trouble even getting him into the Heron sedan."

"Because he won't fit?"

"Oh no, that's not the problem. I thought I had told you before that he doesn't like to ride in cars, and he will only do it if I'm driving, or Saul Panzer, who I know you've met."

"Yes, a couple of times on my visits to you. He seems like a fine gentleman."

"He is, although I'd never tell him that. And he's also a good poker player—too good, as far as I'm concerned. He's taking over some of my duties back home while I'm lollygagging around here."

"*Lollygagging*? Is that what we are doing now?"

"I suppose you could call it that, but for what it's worth, I'm finding my time here to be a very pleasant change of pace."

"I am happy to hear that, Archie. I thought you might find yourself bored once you got away from the Mulgrew business."

"I'm rarely if ever bored, Mom. Besides, it's good for me to be away from Wolfe and the brownstone on occasion. We tend to get on each other's nerves; and also, he needs to see what things are like for him when I'm not around."

"Aren't you afraid that Mr. Panzer might take your place permanently?"

"No, as good as Saul is, he would never want to be Nero Wolfe's full-time assistant. He's got a thriving business himself as an investigator, which he would never give up. I doubt if he's spending more than a day and a half a week, if that, at my desk in the brownstone."

"Well, as long as you can spare the time, I'm happy to have you around."

"I always make it a point to be away from New York for at least a week or two every year, sometimes more. Lily and I have taken quite a few trips together, to Europe, the Caribbean, and to the ranch she owns up in Montana.

"There is a feeling on the part of too many New Yorkers that they live in the center of the country, if not the world, and that everything else revolves around them and their city," I continued. "Now I don't happen to feel that way, even after having lived in Manhattan for so long. But still, I feel it's important for me to remind myself of how diverse this country is, and how many people in it don't give a damn what's going on in that place that likes to refer to itself as 'The Big Apple.'"

"I have sensed New York's pleased view of itself when I've been there," my mother said. "Not from you, or Mr. Wolfe, or from our dear Lily. I'm glad that you're not yet homesick for the hustle and bustle and the neon lights."

Before setting out this morning, I had consulted my Ohio road map and confirmed that the state fairgrounds lay north and east of Columbus's downtown. We arrived there well before ten and went straight to where the quilts were displayed.

"These are impressive," I said to my mother as we looked at the dozens of quilts displayed on the walls in the exhibition hall. "But then, so are yours. Have you ever entered any at the state fair?"

"Oh, my, no!" she said, brushing the idea aside with a sniff. "I'm just not in the same class with these people. I am a county-level quilter, and the work you see here is by some of the best in the whole country. I recognize a few of the names here as people from Iowa, Minnesota, Vermont, and other places whom I've read about in my quilting magazines. These are the very best of the best."

"I hope you're enjoying yourself."

"I really am, and I've picked up a few ideas that I'm going to try out at home."

"I'm glad to hear that," I said, meaning it. After spending an hour and a half looking at the array of quilts, we left the fairgrounds and stopped for lunch at a restaurant near the state capitol, a building my mother ruefully remarked that she hadn't seen for "at least forty years."

"There's really no reason for you to come up here," I told her. "It seems to me you have a rich life right there at home. You don't appear to be sitting alone in your house doing nothing."

"I really do try to keep busy, Archie, and I have a lot of people whom I consider to be good friends. I think my sister envies me that."

"She should. She seems a little too interested in what people are up to, including maybe some things they shouldn't be up to."

"Don't be too hard on Edna, Archie. She has a good heart, and she also has always been very considerate of me. The last time I came down with the flu—which thankfully doesn't happen often—she came over every day with hot meals and soup and made sure that I had everything else I needed."

"You're right, Mom, sometimes I'm too quick to judge. Nero Wolfe has cautioned me about that."

CHAPTER 23

The next morning, I came downstairs to a pleasant aroma. My mother was making a Denver omelet, which she remembered was a favorite of mine growing up.

"Good morning, Archie, did you sleep well?"

"I did, and that's the very same question Nero Wolfe asks me when he comes down in the elevator every morning after tending to the orchids, or 'his concubines,' as he refers to them."

"Well, after all, I am trying to make you feel at home. You had better take a look at this morning's *Trumpet*, which is at your place at the dining room table. It's like nothing I have ever seen from that newspaper before. For a minute, I thought I was in New York City with those half-sized dailies and their screamer headlines."

"Tabloids, you mean," I said, reaching for the *Trumpet*. I saw what she meant. The across-the-front-page headline, which met Mom's definition of a "screamer," shouted "How Did Logan

Mulgrew Really Die?" The subhead read "An In-depth Report on a Noted Banker's Life and His Mysterious Demise."

Katie Padgett hadn't wasted any time in getting her story into print, no doubt pushed by her new editor, Martin Chase, who was out to make a name for himself. Katie's opening paragraphs, set in oversized type, were worthy of one of those Manhattan tabloids:

> Who killed Logan Mulgrew? That is a question many local residents are asking, despite our police department's continued insistence that the prosperous and cantankerous banker committed suicide. "Suicide, hah!" one local resident scoffed. "Let's face it, Mulgrew was the most hated man in the county, if not the state, and any number of people would have been happy to see him dead."
>
> Other townsfolk, none of whom agreed to be quoted by name, have also stepped forward proclaiming their belief that Mulgrew was murdered. "I'd let you use my name, but then I would be in trouble with the local cops. No thank you!"

The article jumped inside and got really interesting. *This could be a bonanza for lawyers*, I thought, as I began reading. Katie had written relatively short profiles of those who could have had reason to dispatch Mr. Mulgrew. *Pretty gutsy*, I thought. The paper's new editor seemed to be turning the humble *Trumpet* into a small-town version of a grocery store tabloid.

Here are some samples:

> Here, without names, are some of those individuals who had reason to wish Logan Mulgrew ill:

• A local dairy farmer who borrowed from Mulgrew's Farmer's State Bank and could not keep up with the payments and got foreclosed on several years ago. He has been outspoken in his bitterness toward Mulgrew, according to people who have heard him publicly berate the banker. The man declined to comment for this article. He now works as a tenant for the absentee owner of another farm in the county.

• Another local individual started a bank here eight years ago, but it did not last long. That man has attributed its failure to rumormongering on the part of Logan Mulgrew, who vehemently denied the charge. However, other residents have reported hearing stories of how the new bank was undercapitalized, which was never substantiated. This talk is said to have frightened potential depositors away. The owner, who refused to be quoted for this article, was ruined and forced to sell his house. Embittered, he works as a mechanic in a local garage.

• The brother of Logan Mulgrew's wife, Sylvia Mulgrew, has alleged that Mulgrew killed his ailing spouse by giving her an overdose of digitalis, although this was never proven, and her death was certified as that of natural causes. Mrs. Mulgrew's brother, who would not speak to this reporter, has contended that Mulgrew killed his wife because he was emotionally involved with her caregiver.

• This caregiver is a professional nurse Logan Mulgrew hired to look after his wife, who had heart trouble and who also was suffering from senility. While she was serving as a caregiver for Sylvia Mulgrew, this woman, decades younger than Mr. Mulgrew, was frequently seen dining with him. After Mrs. Mulgrew's death, the caregiver moved into an apartment building near the courthouse. Mulgrew was often seen entering that building. When this reporter asked the caregiver the extent of her relationship with Logan Mulgrew, she became agitated and ordered me to leave her residence. The woman currently lives in Charleston, West Virginia.

Another local resident, the father of a young woman who had worked as a secretary for Logan Mulgrew at Farmer's State Bank, has publicly accused Logan Mulgrew of sexually assaulting his daughter, a charge that Mulgrew angrily denied. We have been unable to determine whether the young woman was impregnated, and if so, the result of the pregnancy. The woman in question now resides in a city that this publication will not identify, out of respect for her privacy.

I put down the paper to figuratively catch my breath. I have learned enough about journalism from Lon Cohen at the Gazette in New York, with whom Wolfe and I frequently collaborate, to realize that much of what I was now reading was wildly reckless and patently actionable, although whether any of those mentioned, while not by name, would choose to react remained to be seen. I also wondered how the local police department would respond to the coverage. At least Katie Padgett did go to Chief Blankenship for a comment:

Police Chief Thomas Blankenship continues to insist that Logan Mulgrew committed suicide, and he remains adamant that his department will not undertake any investigation. "This is a cut-and-dried case of suicide," he said. "The man clearly was devastated by his wife's long suffering and her death."

When I asked Chief Blankenship if he was concerned that the caregiver had moved out of state and had not been mentioned in Mulgrew's will, he replied, "I see neither of those as factors to be the least bit concerned about. Your newspaper is making a mountain out of a molehill."

The *Trumpet*'s coverage did not stop there. It also carried an editorial headlined "Mountain or Molehill?" in which the writer stressed the newspaper's commitment to continuing its probing:

So it is that our police chief, for whom we have the highest regard, says the *Trumpet* is barking up the wrong tree in our investigation into the deaths of two prominent citizens, Logan and Sylvia Mulgrew. We concede the possibility that Sylvia Mulgrew may have died a natural death. We are far less sanguine about the demise of her husband. Understand this: We are well aware that Logan Mulgrew was a long way from being the most revered individual in our community.

However, are we to become outraged only when beloved people are murdered? The answer is a resounding *no*! And our readers should be assured that this newspaper will continue to investigate the circumstances of Mr. Mulgrew's death until we are satisfied that justice has been done.

The moment I set the *Trumpet* down, the telephone rang. "Hello, Edna," my mother said into the instrument. "Yes, yes, I have read it. Yes, Archie has, too. Would you like to speak to him? It's your aunt," she said, handing me the receiver.

"Hello, Archie. Your mother tells me that you have read today's paper. What do you think?"

"I'm digesting it all, along with my breakfast. It will be interesting to see how the community reacts to this newly crusading *Trumpet*."

"Well, I have already gotten several reactions myself," Edna said. "Four members of my bridge club have telephoned me this morning, and their reactions are mixed."

"Tell me about those reactions."

"Two of them think the paper has gone too far. One said, 'The *Trumpet* has overnight turned into nothing more than a scandal sheet, looking to dig up dirt as a way to sell newspapers.' Another agreed, telling me she was going to write a letter to the editor, saying she would drop her subscription if this was the kind of irresponsible writing they were going to be doing."

"And how about the other two, those who liked the coverage?"

"One thought that it was about time somebody told the story of that young so-called caregiver, who of course is Carrie Yeager. 'That woman is a slattern, the way she flaunted her relationship with Mr. Mulgrew. It was clear to him that when he saw her for what she was, a gold digger, he dropped her like a hot potato, and then in her anger, she shot him.'"

"That is quite an indictment," I told Edna. "And I will have to look up the meaning of *slattern*, although I'm pretty sure I know what it means. What do you think of Miss Yeager yourself?"

"As you know, Archie, I try to not be judgmental," my aunt said as I suppressed a laugh. "But I must say that I was suspicious of her from the moment I heard that Logan had died of a gunshot."

"The way the *Trumpet* has put together its coverage, Carrie Yeager has been made to seem suspicious at best, guilty at worst," I commented.

"That is hardly surprising, the way she behaved," Edna said

with a sniff of small-town disapproval. "I would not be at all surprised if our police chief doesn't change his mind and see Logan's death as what it appears to be—a murder."

"One thing is certain," I said. "Chief Blankenship will be under pressure to take some sort of action after what's been printed."

CHAPTER 24

The next call to the house came as no surprise to me. "It's Katie Padgett," my mother said, again giving me the receiver. "I appreciate your handling my calls," I told her as I cupped the mouthpiece.

"Hi, Katie, you have certainly been one busy young lady."

"What did you think of it all, Archie?' she asked in an anxious tone.

"I must say I have mixed feelings. It's quite a package, and I am glad to see the *Trumpet* is not buying Blankenship's position. But it seems like the paper has opened itself up to all sorts of lawsuits, in the areas of both libel and privacy, although I am no expert on press law. Also, it looks like you are trying to drop a noose over Carrie Yeager's head, to use a phrase."

"How can you say that?"

"You certainly did not portray her in a very good light."

"She does not deserve to be put in a very good light, Archie. After all, you were there when I interviewed her in Charleston."

"Has Blankenship called you? He must have seen the paper by now."

"He telephoned Marty, not me."

"That would be Martin Chase, your crusading young editor, right?"

"Don't be sarcastic, Archie. Yes, the chief called him, and he was mad as hell. He said the *Trumpet* was behaving, and I quote, 'like one of those big-city tabloids, the kind that you would find in New York or Chicago.'"

"He does have a point there. Did he also indicate that he would begin a murder investigation, based on today's issue?"

"Marty asked him that question and was told that our coverage has done nothing whatever to change his mind."

"Is it too early to ask what kind of reaction the *Trumpet* is getting from its readers?"

"No, Archie, and that's really exciting. Marty figured there would be plenty of reaction, and he brought in two operators to run our small switchboard, starting at eight o'clock. They can't keep up with the calls."

"Did he tell you how the pros and cons were running?"

"Yes, I talked to him just before I called you, and he said people who didn't approve of what we wrote were outnumbering the ones who liked it by about two to one."

"That must not make him very happy."

"On the contrary. Marty says it's okay to get people angry as long as they talk about you. And right now, he says that we are the talk of the town."

"I am sure you are. But you may be the talk of the legal community, as well."

"Marty says it's possible we might get sued by somebody who we've written about, but he claims that's the risk one takes when one stakes out a strong position. Oh, and one other thing: People have been streaming into the office off the street buying copies of the paper at the front counter, several dozen folks so far. One woman bought four copies, another took three, and others took more than one. I'm told that has almost never happened before."

"Do you have any idea how the *Trumpet's* owners feel about all this notoriety?"

"I don't, Archie. The editor, if you want to call him that, is Mr. Ferguson, who doesn't do any editing. He's really the publisher and owner, and he's the one who okayed hiring Marty. I've heard that some of the other newsroom people who have to report to Marty think he's too rash and impulsive. But I happen to think he's just what the paper needs to be relevant."

"You could be right about that, but I happen to believe both Blankenship and your boss are wrong."

"What do you mean?"

"Blankenship is wrong in believing Mulgrew's death was a suicide, and the *Trumpet* is wrong in pushing for Carrie Yeager as his killer."

"Okay, then do you care to nominate a killer?"

"I do not."

"Well, Archie, we will just have to see how it all plays out. I for one think this is incredibly energizing," Katie said in a smug tone. "And after all, we did not use any names."

"You really didn't have to," I said. "The great majority of your readers will be able to recognize each of the so-called suspects by the way they were described. As I said earlier, I don't claim to know anything about libel laws, but I will be surprised if somebody doesn't sue the *Trumpet* over this story."

"Marty says that we and our lawyers will be ready for them," Katie replied.

I couldn't think of a response to that, so I just told her that I had to take my mother shopping and we hung up.

"I'm sorry to have been eavesdropping, Archie, but I don't have to go shopping."

"I know you don't, but I'd had enough of the girl reporter for now. This Mulgrew business is not going well." I then repeated to her what I'd told Katie about both Blankenship and the *Trumpet* being on the wrong track.

"So you believe Logan Mulgrew was murdered, and that the Yeager woman is not his killer?"

"That's it, Mom," I said, leaning back and shaking my head. "But I can't figure out who did the killing, and it scares the daylights out of me that Carrie Yeager might end up getting nailed for it.

"Factor number one: Blankenship may be both earnest and honest; but brilliant he is not, and stubborn he is. He has claimed so often that Mulgrew killed himself that now he can't bear to admit that he could be wrong. He doesn't want to lose face.

"Factor number two: This hotshot new editor of the *Trumpet* wants to be able to crack the case and claim some glory. And Katie, who's also looking for some glory, has been pushing Carrie Yeager as the killer."

My mother sat at the dining room table with me and poured a fresh cup of coffee for each of us from the pot. "What makes you think Miss Yeager didn't do the shooting, Archie?"

"I can't explain it, Mom. It's just a feeling I've got. If Nero Wolfe were here, he would probably figure it all out like that," I said, snapping my fingers. "But at the risk of stating the obvious, I am no Nero Wolfe, not by a country mile. Other than getting the chance to spend time with you, which has been delightful, I don't know why I came down here. Well . . . yes I do. I was too damned full of myself, and when dear Aunt Edna laid out her suspicions about Mulgrew's death, I thought I would just wade in and find the shooter within a day or two. Well, you now see the result of my pride . . ."

"I'm glad you came, but I'm sorry that things have turned out this way. What do you plan to do now?"

"I think, if you don't mind, I'll hang around for a couple more days, if only to see how this business plays out. If nothing else, it will be interesting to see the community's reaction to the *Trumpet* coverage, which I gather so far from Aunt Edna and Katie has been mixed."

"Why would I mind, for heaven's sake? This is the longest you've stayed here with me in years, and I happen to be enjoying it."

"Even though you've turned into a glorified telephone answerer for me?" My mother didn't have time to respond, because, as if on cue, the instrument rang.

"Hello? Oh yes, Chief, yes. That will be all right. And he does happen to be here now."

She hung up and turned to me. "As I'm sure you could tell, that was Chief Blankenship. He's coming over, and he wanted to be sure you were around."

"That spells trouble of some sort. All right, I will gird myself and prepare for the worst."

Fifteen minutes later, the doorbell rang, and Mom admitted the police chief in his crisply pressed uniform. "Please come in," she said. "I am just brewing a fresh pot of coffee."

"Thank you, Mrs. Goodwin. I am sorry to intrude, but I felt this visit was necessary." Blankenship sat on the living room sofa as directed, and my mother served him coffee as I walked in. "Good morning, Chief," I said, taking a chair facing him.

"I don't happen to think this is such a good morning," the policeman said, his square-jawed face locked in a grim expression. "I am sure you've had a chance to read the paper."

"We both have," Mom said as she sat and eyed Blankenship. "What do you think?"

"I think the coverage is a disgrace," he said. "And I'm sorry to say this, Mrs. Goodwin, but I lay a large part of the blame on your son."

"Really? And just why is that, Chief Blankenship?"

"He has been a bad influence on that young reporter. He's been a real Svengali."

"As a onetime English teacher, I am glad to learn that you must have read Mr. du Maurier's novel *Trilby*, but I can hardly see my son in the role of that controlling, manipulating fictional character you mentioned."

"Don't be too sure of that. It seems that since Mr. Goodwin arrived in town, Katie Padgett has been energized to the point that she is determined to stir up trouble over the death of Logan Mulgrew."

"If I may put my two cents' worth in," I said, "you should know that I have had almost nothing to do with Miss Padgett's reporting. She is now being spurred on by that new young editor at the *Trumpet*."

"That may very well be," Blankenship said, "but you also seem to have taken a great interest in Mr. Mulgrew's death. I continue to believe your presence here is an unsettling factor. Now I know the limits of my authority, and I realize that I can't force you to leave, but I really wish you would, for the overall good of the community."

"Chief Blankenship, I gather that you continue to believe Logan Mulgrew killed himself," I said.

"I do. And I gather that you continue to believe he was murdered. Do you have a suspect in mind?"

"No, it could be one of several people."

"That is far from helpful, Mr. Goodwin. It would appear that the *Trumpet* would have us believe, although they did not use her name, that the caregiver is the most likely suspect. How do you feel about that?"

"I don't believe it."

"All right. Tell me why you think Mulgrew was killed."

"By all accounts, the man seemed to be enjoying life, and there did not appear to be any indication that he was devastated by his wife's death. Although I do not subscribe to the *Trumpet's* somewhat breathless tabloid treatment of the Mulgrew story, it seems to me they did a fairly thorough job of suggesting people—and not just Miss Yeager—who had strong reasons to dislike the banker. It seems clear that you do not agree."

"No one has yet to show me a compelling case for murder. Or a compelling case for any one individual as the killer, for that matter," Blankenship said, rising. "Thank you for the coffee, Mrs. Goodwin. I hope to continue seeing you around town, in less-tense circumstances."

It was obvious that, by "less-tense circumstances," Blankenship meant with me no longer present in the community.

CHAPTER 25

"The chief seems to be under a great deal of strain," my mother observed after Blankenship had left.

"Without question. I think he is seriously beginning to doubt his contention about suicide."

"I believe that is the real reason that he came today, Archie, not to urge you to leave. He respects your opinion, and he was hoping you might have some definite idea about a murderer."

"If that was the case, I'm sorry to have disappointed him. If nothing else, I was firm in my rejection of Carrie Yeager as the killer. I'm good at saying who *didn't* do the killing. I just can't figure out who did. I'm no help to anybody."

"Now, Archie, that is not true, and you know it. Right now, you are the balance beam between a man who believes nobody killed Logan Mulgrew and a woman who is positive she knows who killed him."

"And what good does that do me? As I said before, I think I'll just stay around for another day or two to see what the *Trumpet* has up its sleeve, and then head back to New York."

To get my mind off the case, I decided to drive around the area with the top down on the convertible. I invited my mother to come along, but she said she had lots of tasks around the house. Only later did I learn what was going on.

My spin on that sunny June afternoon took me to as many of my old haunts as I could think of—or remember. Both my elementary school and high school looked pretty much like I remembered them, although each building seemed somehow smaller than when I had walked their halls. And I was sorry to see that the old minor league baseball park was gone, replaced by a one-story factory building that manufactured ball bearings, according to a sign out in front. I reminded myself to ask my mother if the town still had a team and, if so, where it played its games.

The county park with its swimming pool and the pond where you could rent a rowboat was still there. My first date had been in one of those boats, and I remember impressing the girl with how skillfully I could handle the oars. What she didn't know was that I had gone out alone twice to practice rowing. The last thing any teenage boy wants is to be embarrassed the first time he is with a girl. And I was damned if I was going to make a fool of myself in front of Eleanor Ann Cochran, who my friend Spud said was the prettiest girl in the high school. And I agreed.

Years later when I told Lily Rowan that I had gone out with the most beautiful girl in my school, she replied, "Well, isn't that nice. You have come a long way. Now you go out with the most beautiful woman in New York City." She had me there; I couldn't, and wouldn't, deny it.

The rest of my drive proved that, as somebody once wrote, you can't go home again. Well, technically you *can*, but it is never the same.

When I got back to the house in the late afternoon, I suggested to my mother that we revisit the local Italian restaurant and she agreed, not having begun preparations for dinner. I found her to be unusually reserved as we ate, which I attributed to the turmoil surrounding the Mulgrew case. My coming home had definitely been a mixed blessing for her.

The next morning before breakfast, I paged through the *Trumpet* and was surprised at the lack of coverage of the Mulgrew business. Oh, there was a piece on page one by Katie that quoted "Our local newspaper seems determined to make a case for the murder of Logan Mulgrew where none exists. I have nothing further to say on the subject." The only other mentions were two letters from readers, one pro, one con.

"I am shocked that the *Trumpet* would lower itself to this sort of scandalmongering," wrote Mrs. L. Williams, while Jonathan Schmidt commented, "I am delighted to see that your newspaper has tackled a serious issue." Lon Cohen had told me once that it was important for a paper to follow up a big story on the second day with more information, "to keep the momentum going," as he put it. The *Trumpet* seemed to lose momentum on day number two, for whatever reason.

Mom still seemed distracted at breakfast, with little interest in the newspaper. I was tempted to ask what was troubling her, but thought better of it; I wasn't sure I wanted to know the answer.

Her mood continued throughout the day, even in the grocery store, where I drove her, and by midafternoon, she was looking out of the window every few minutes. Then at just after four, I saw something out of that same window that made me blink.

A sedan pulled into the driveway, and not just any sedan. It was a royal blue Heron, and lest there be any confusion about its owner, the car carried the familiar black-numerals-on-orange-background license plates that marked it as being from the state of New York.

I stepped outside in time to see the big car ease to a stop. The driver's side door opened, and out stepped one Saul Panzer, all five feet seven of him, wearing the familiar flat cap and with a day-old beard on a face that was two-thirds nose. He nodded to me with a lopsided grin.

If I thought that was a shock, and it was, there was a bigger one to come, both literally and figuratively. Like a good chauffeur, Saul held open the back door and out stepped none other than Nero Wolfe, clad in a three-piece suit with a yellow shirt and a brown-and-yellow tie. He wore a sour expression and carried an applewood walking stick.

"Well, what are you gaping at?" he demanded, glaring in the same way he often does when I have said or done something he does not agree with.

"For starters, I'm more than mildly surprised that you have chosen to grace the provinces with your presence. Dare I ask how the journey was?"

He responded with something that sounded like a growl and said, "May we go inside? I would like to sit, for the first time in hours, in something that is not in motion."

"By all means, let's go in," I said as Saul, behind Wolfe, kept on grinning.

"Hello, Mr. Wolfe," my mother said as we stepped into the kitchen. She avoided my look and turned away. I was beginning to figure things out.

"Mrs. Goodwin," Wolfe said, bowing slightly. "Thank you in advance for your hospitality."

"I am happy to host you. And you, too, Mr. Panzer. It has been some time since we have seen each other."

Saul took off his cap and smiled. "I am planning to get a room at one of the local hotels, Mrs. Goodwin."

"You will do no such thing!" Mom told him. "This is a big house with plenty of bedrooms upstairs, and they sit empty other than on those too-rare occasions when my children and/ or grandchildren deign to come for a visit. I will show both of you to your rooms. Archie, you can bring their luggage in."

"Everything is in the trunk," Saul said, tossing me the keys. Nice to know I had been given a role. I carted in Wolfe's large leather suitcase, which he had taken when we went to Montenegro in search of a killer,* as well as Saul's smaller bag and a big cooler, which I opened and found to contain more than two dozen bottles of Remmers beer, along with a stein and a bottle opener. Wolfe had come prepared.

I carried the suitcases upstairs and learned that Mom had put Wolfe in the big corner bedroom and Saul in a smaller one next door. Like a good porter, I put their suitcases in the proper rooms and then began to fill the refrigerator with the bottles of beer.

As I finished with those little chores, Mom came into the kitchen. I turned and said, "All right, just what—"

"Before you start in on me, Archie, hear me out," she said, holding up a hand as if in self-defense. "Yes, I took it upon myself, without asking you, to telephone Mr. Wolfe and tell him about the situation here, at least as well as I have figured it out. He listened patiently and then said, to my surprise, 'I will discuss this with Mr. Panzer.'"

---

* *The Black Mountain* by Rex Stout

"You can imagine my surprise when he called me back and asked if he could come here and stay in this house. He said Mr. Panzer could drive him. It has always been my understanding that Nero Wolfe will go to great lengths to avoid leaving his brownstone."

"I am every bit as surprised as you are. Did you ask him to come?"

"No, as I said, I thought that maybe he might have some advice for you."

"And you figured I would be too proud to ask him, right?"

"Well . . ."

"All right, Mom, what is done is done, and I am not about to dwell on it. I'm still getting over the shock of seeing Wolfe climb out of that car. He probably drove Saul crazy during the trip."

"Aw, he wasn't really all that bad, Archie," Saul said, surprising us as he stepped into the kitchen. "Although he did hold on to that strap pretty tightly most of the way, especially when we went through those tunnels on the Pennsylvania Turnpike. I don't think I went over the speed limit once on the whole trip, or we would have gotten here sooner."

"You deserve a medal," I told him. "Did he complain a lot?"

"Not really, although his expressions, as seen through the rearview mirror, varied from anger to terror. The one good part of the trip was when we pulled off the road at a rest stop and had a delicious picnic of cold chicken and a Waldorf salad that Fritz had prepared."

"So at least he has been fed, which is good to know. I suppose I had better go up and see how he's doing after his harrowing voyage," I said. "Wish me luck."

The door to what for now was Wolfe's room was open, and I looked in. He sat in a chair that could accommodate his bulk—barely—and was reading a book.

"Can I get you anything, beer perhaps?"

He looked up and dipped his chin slightly—a nod. I went to the kitchen, where Mom and Saul were talking, and took two chilled beers and the stein from the refrigerator, putting everything on a tray, along with an opener. I then went back upstairs and, doing my best Fritz Brenner impression, placed the presentation on a small table next to Wolfe. I got another nod for a thanks.

"I take it you are comfortable."

"Comfortable enough," Wolfe grumped.

"Glad to hear it. Before we get to business, as I believe we ultimately will, I know you have started thinking about dinner. I will just say this to you: don't worry; you will be pleasantly surprised."

As I began to catch up with all that had been happening under my nose, I realized based on the items Mom had gotten at the grocery store that she was planning to serve pork tenderloin in casserole again. At the time, I thought it odd she would have the same meal twice in the space of a few days, but now I realized what was going on. She had mastered this dish, which she again served with carrots, celery, and onions, and she hoped the menu and the preparation would measure up to Wolfe's high standards.

I left the man to his book and his beer and went downstairs to help with the dinner for the four of us.

CHAPTER 26

Back downstairs, I found Saul Panzer in the living room with what he told me was scotch and water over ice. "I didn't even know Mom had scotch around," I remarked.

"All I had to do was ask. She told me she keeps all sorts of libations for guests. And by the way, this happens to be a fine label," he said, raising his glass in a salute.

"Well, after the day you have had, you're entitled to a drink, or maybe more than one."

As we were talking, my mother came in and asked me, "When do you have dinner in the brownstone?"

"Usually seven fifteen, sometimes seven thirty. Why?"

"I want to make Mr. Wolfe feel at home, and because we are in the same time zone as New York, he will be able to eat at the usual hour."

"Really, Mom, don't you think you're overindulging him?"

"I believe you told me once that your boss has said, if I remember the quote, 'a guest is a jewel on the cushion of hospitality.' And after all, Mr. Wolfe is a guest in my house, as are you, Mr. Panzer."

"Well, I for one have never been called a jewel before, but, hey, I kind of like the sound of it," Saul said.

"Oh brother, now see what you've started, Mom? You're going to spoil these two guys rotten."

"And why shouldn't I? They are here to help, are they not?"

"Yes, but just don't go overboard, or they'll take advantage of your cushion of hospitality."

"Seems like a pretty comfortable cushion to me," Saul said.

"See, Mom, the smugness has already set in. And if you think Mr. Panzer here is fussy, just wait till Nero Wolfe begins to demand things."

"Oh, pshaw," she said, waving my concern away with a hand. "I am sure that they will prove to be perfect guests."

"Of course, we will," Saul piped up.

"Okay, just don't say I didn't warn you," I told my mother.

The meal was a great success, and if Wolfe was surprised at the quality of my mother's cooking, he didn't show it. He had two full helpings of the pork, as did Saul. And as he always does in the brownstone, Wolfe set the conversation topic, which this night was the history of Ohio.

"Mrs. Goodwin, I am sure I do not have to tell you that this very community we are in was an early capital of the territory before Ohio became a state," Wolfe said.

"No, I was well aware of that," my mother said. "Most of the early growth was in the southern part of the state because of all the traffic on the Ohio River before there were decent roads."

Well, that set the two of them off, and they spent the rest of the meal, including Mom's strawberries Romanoff (which I know she also learned about from Fritz Brenner), swapping facts about Ohio's history, including many I never learned in school or else had long forgotten.

After dinner, she surprised me yet again by giving Wolfe, Saul, and me cognac, in snifters no less, and then poured some for herself. The brandy was not Remisier, that nectar Wolfe serves at home to special guests. But to my semitrained palate, what we were sipping seemed more than adequate, and apparently Wolfe thought so, too.

"Mrs. Goodwin, this has been an elegant dinner," he said. "I would like to reciprocate tomorrow, although it will necessitate a visit to one or more groceries. I will prepare a list and of course pay for the ingredients."

"You will not pay a single penny," my mother replied. "I will welcome your presence in my kitchen and I will be happy to learn from you, as I have learned from Mr. Brenner on my visits to New York."

"We will talk tomorrow," Wolfe said. "At present, I need to spend some time with Archie. We have a great deal to discuss."

"Mrs. Goodwin, do you know how to play gin rummy?" Saul asked. "I would be happy to teach you."

"I played it for years with my late husband, Mr. Panzer, and I think I can remember everything I need to."

"Just remember not to play him for money, Mom," I said as Wolfe and I went up to his room.

"Sorry there's no elevator here," I said as he settled into the easy chair my mother had hauled in from one of the other bedrooms. "But I think you can handle a single flight of stairs."

He drew in a bushel of air and let it out slowly, ignoring my comment. "It sounds as if you are flummoxed, am I correct?"

"That is as good a word as any," I conceded.

"Very well. Report."

What he said in that single word was that he wanted me to recite every conversation I had taken part in relating to Logan Mulgrew's death since my arrival in Ohio. If that sounds like a tall order, it is. But Nero Wolfe was well aware that I possessed what one of my high school teachers had referred to as "total recall"—that is, the ability to repeat, verbatim, long stretches of dialogue. It was possibly the only quality I possessed that Wolfe envied.

"This is going to take a while," I told him. "I'll get you some beer."

Once Wolfe had started in on the first of the two bottles of Remmers I had brought up, he nodded for me to begin. As I was downstairs getting his beer, I quickly calculated that I had talked to nine people about Mulgrew, some of them more than once.

I began with Aunt Edna, who had been the trigger, more or less, of the whole damned business. What ensued over the next ninety minutes was the longest recitation of this kind I had ever done. Wolfe interrupted me no more than a half-dozen times, and then only with brief questions.

"Well, that is it," I told him, spreading my arms, palms up. "I am now an empty vessel." He did not respond, and for a moment I thought he was going to start in on that exercise of his where he closes his eyes, and pulls his lips in and pushes them out, again and again.

When that happens, and it has taken anywhere from less than a minute to more than a half hour, Wolfe ends by opening his eyes as if he had been asleep and he invariably has come up with a solution to whatever mystery we had been working on. Such was not to be the case now, however.

"I am going to bed," he stated. It was then I realized how tired I was, and how dry my mouth was from all the yapping I had done. I wished him a good night, closed the door behind me, and went down to the kitchen for a glass of milk.

CHAPTER 27

The next morning, I was shocked again by the *Trumpet*. It did not carry a single word about the Mulgrew death. Could it be a lawsuit had been filed, and that the editors were lying low?

My mother, in her determination to cater to Wolfe, had prepared a breakfast tray for him and took it up to his room, apparently making sure he was treated like the aforementioned jewel on a cushion of hospitality.

"How did your game go last night?" I asked Saul as he came down and sat at the dining room coffee table, pouring himself a cup of coffee.

"Your mom's good, did you know that?"

"I never played cards with her, but I can remember as a kid hearing her and my father playing, and it seemed like she cried 'Gin!' a lot."

"Well, she cried 'Gin!' a lot last night, too. The evening ended up pretty much in a draw."

"That's better than I usually do against you. And I'll bet she hasn't played in years, unless one of her church groups has a gin rummy table. But I know that she does play a lot of bridge."

"That's a tough game," Saul said. "It's got to sharpen her card sense."

"What has got to sharpen my card sense?" Mom asked as she came into the room.

"Playing bridge," I told her. "I understand you gave Saul a rough time with the cards."

"Oh, I think he must have won in the end," she declared. "He plays very well."

"As I have found, much to my regret," I said. "How is my boss doing this morning?"

"He was very polite when I delivered his breakfast. I think he was happy with it."

"What did you give him?"

"Coffee, of course, orange juice, fresh peaches, blueberry muffins, hashed brown potatoes, an omelet, and broiled ham."

"Did it occur to you that if he stays a few days, he will come to expect this kind of treatment every morning?"

"And he will get this kind of treatment every morning, Archie. He has come here to help you, and that is the very least I can do."

"See, Saul, what I have to bear up under—a mother who is truly a saint."

"Archie, stop it! Mr. Panzer doesn't want to listen to that kind of talk."

"Please call me Saul. I can't think of anybody else who starts my name with a 'Mister.'"

"All right, Saul it is," Mom said, laughing. "Mr. Wolfe—or should I now refer to him as Nero?—has given me a list of groceries to get for a meal he is preparing tonight. He suggested you might be available to drive me, as I understand he and Archie will want to talk this morning."

"It would be my pleasure," Saul said.

"Off the two of you go, then," I told them. "I've got business of my own."

My business consisted of a call to Katie Padgett, to find out what was going on at the *Trumpet*. She answered after a couple of rings, "Padgett, newsroom."

"Goodwin, Portsmouth Road."

"Archie! I didn't expect to hear from you. I know you're miffed about some of what I've been writing."

"Speaking of what you have been writing, I didn't see a single word about Mulgrew in today's edition. What's going on at the paper?"

"Somebody, I don't know who, has filed a suit against us, and the owner of the paper sent down an order that until we hear from him or her, nothing more can be written about Mulgrew's death. We can't even run any letters from readers about it."

"Who do you think is behind the suit?"

"If I were to guess, I would lay odds it's that damned Carrie Yeager. Oh, I know what you're going to say, Archie. You think that I am out to get her."

"I'm going to reserve judgment for now. What does the *Trumpet*'s new young editor think of this development?"

"As you can guess, he's not very happy. 'I thought I was coming to a paper that wanted to shake things up,' he told me. 'But now it looks like this place is as spineless as other dailies that I've worked on.'"

"Do you think he will quit?"

"I hope not, but he might. And here I thought I was getting a great opportunity to show what I can do. This doesn't seem fair. I feel like the rug's been pulled out from under me."

"Maybe you're being tested to see how you respond to adversity," I said, not really believing it.

Katie's own "maybe" in response lacked conviction, and we ended the call.

I then went up to Wolfe's room and found him reading a book, *The Sea Around Us*, by Rachel Carson.

"I understand you are doing the cooking tonight," I told him.

Looking up, he said, "Do you find that surprising?"

"Not in the least. I am eagerly anticipating whatever you come up with. Mom and Saul are out right now getting your ingredients."

Wolfe started to go back to his book, but I was not done. "I went through today's *Trumpet*, and they didn't carry a single word on the Mulgrew death, so I called Katie Padgett. She tells me a lawsuit has been filed, and the owner of the paper has ordered that there be no more coverage of the case until further notice."

"A lawsuit is hardly surprising, given the slipshod journalism the publication indulges in, as based on that issue you showed me," Wolfe said. "Mr. Cohen of the *Gazette* would be appalled, despite the aggressive journalism his newspaper often practices."

"Yeah, the *Gazette* is tough but fair. What is our next move?"

"It is always wiser, given the choice, to trust to inertia; it is the greatest force in the world."

"I've heard those words, or similar ones, from you before. I gather you have not yet developed a plan."

"Gather what you will, Archie. I am in no mood today for impetuosity."

"Heaven forbid that you should ever be impetuous. I know your book must be fascinating, so I will leave you to it," I said, resisting the temptation to slam the door behind me on the way out.

CHAPTER 28

On the one hand, I was both surprised and pleased that Nero Wolfe had gone against the grain, traveling several hundred miles in an automobile, an almost unthinkable and reckless enterprise for him. On the other hand, I was frustrated with his inertia, to use the man's own term.

I was hired by Wolfe years ago at least in part to serve as a burr under his saddle. He knows damned well that he often needs to be goaded into action, and I see myself as the goader-in-chief. It can be a thankless task, however, because he is every bit as stubborn as I am. At this time, I saw us as being in a war of wills—a war that I was determined to win.

I was back downstairs when my mother and Saul came in carrying a bunch of bulging grocery bags. "Well, that was interesting," she said.

"What was interesting, Mom?"

"We were at Kroger's, in the meat department, when who did we run into but your aunt Edna."

"Uh-oh."

"Yes, uh-oh. As will not surprise you, she was very curious as to why I was with Saul. I had no choice but to introduce them to each other, and she said, 'Saul Panzer, my, what an unusual name. And where do you happen to be from, Mr. Panzer?'

"Saul, bless him, let me do all the talking. So I told Edna that Saul was staying with us, along with Nero Wolfe. And I wish you could have seen her eyes—bigger than saucers, they were. I'm sorry that I let the cat out of the bag, but I did not feel that I had any other choice."

"You really didn't, Mom."

"And now, of course, thanks to our family's very own town crier, word will be all over town and throughout the county that Mr. Wolfe is here."

"It was bound to happen sooner or later, Mrs. Goodwin," Saul said. "Maybe that's not such a bad thing."

"I agree with Saul," I said. "It saves us having to pussyfoot around until Wolfe finally starts kicking his gray matter into high gear. By the way, what's he making for dinner tonight?"

"Planked porterhouse steak," Mom said. "Saul and I were able to get a fine cut, two inches thick as specified by Mr. Wolfe, to be served with mashed potatoes, mushrooms, and slices of fresh lime. Fortunately, I have an oak cooking plank that I haven't used in ages."

"I've eaten Wolfe's planked steak, although not for several years, and I can tell you that we are all in for a fine dinner tonight," I said. "Even Fritz Brenner, who does not always approve of the dishes his boss cooks, has praised this one."

Mom and Saul put away the groceries and gave me two out-of-town newspapers I had requested for Wolfe, the *New*

York Times and the *Chicago Tribune,* the *New York Gazette* not being available at the local magazine and cigar shop; I took them up to him and said, "The grocery items you requested have been purchased and will be ready for you—after lunch, of course." He gave me his version of a nod and began tackling the newspapers.

"Oh, and speaking of lunch, it will be served at one, chicken with mushrooms and tarragon." Another nod. He really was resting on that cushion of hospitality, thanks to my overindulgent mother.

I went down to the living room and sat with my last cup of coffee of the morning, wondering who would be the first to call as word of Wolfe being in town got around. I gave odds of three-to-two for Katie Padgett, two-to-one for Aunt Edna, and three-to-one for Police Chief Blankenship.

Twenty minutes later, I declared myself a winner. "Telephone for you, Archie," my mother said, handing me the receiver and stretching the cord as far as it would reach.

"Hello, Archie," Katie Padgett said in a decidedly cool tone. "I understand there is a newsworthy visitor in your mother's house."

"It depends on how you define newsworthy," I responded.

"Well, I define the most-famous private detective in America as being newsworthy," she said in a snappish tone.

"Actually, I believe Nero Wolfe would prefer to be referred to as the most-famous private detective in the *world.*"

"Have it your way, Archie. Why does he happen to be here?"

"I'm curious by nature. How did you learn that he's in town?"

"That's unimportant. Answer me."

"I think you can guess the answer to your own question."

"This is big news, Archie. I need to interview him, and as soon as possible."

"Sorry, but I can speak for Mr. Wolfe when I say he is not available to the press."

"Then I will write that he is here to investigate Logan Mulgrew's death and refuses to comment."

"Really? I thought your bosses had declared a moratorium on articles about the Mulgrew death. How are you going to get around that?" The silence on the other end continued for several seconds.

"I'll . . . figure something out," she finally replied, which told me that she felt stymied, at least for the moment. "Good-bye, Archie," she said before I heard the click. I had been dismissed, but I knew I had not heard the last of the intrepid young female reporter.

I barely had time to finish my coffee when the phone squawked again, and my mother answered. She was getting used to the traffic over the wire.

"Yes, yes, he is right here," she said, handing me the receiver and rolling her eyes. "It's Chief Blankenship."

"Goodwin speaking," I said.

"Tom Blankenship." I waited for him to say more, but no words were forthcoming. Finally, I broke the silence. "Yes, sir?"

"You know of course why I'm calling."

"I am not sure that I do."

"Don't try to get cute with me, Mr. Goodwin. Let's get straight to the point, shall we?"

"By all means."

"I have heard that Nero Wolfe is in town, and that he is staying at your mother's house. Is that true?"

"It is."

"Just why is he here?"

"I will answer a question with a question, Chief. Is he being accused of breaking a law?"

"Of course not, but it seems most unusual that a famous—make that *legendary*—private investigator from New York has chosen to spend time in what to him must seem like a very small community. I would like to talk to Mr. Wolfe."

"I certainly will tell him of your desire, but knowing him, I can't guarantee that he will wish to speak to you, unless there is an extremely good reason."

"It is my belief that he is here to investigate the gunshot death of Logan Mulgrew."

"A death you have steadfastly claimed to be a suicide."

"You are correct."

"Such being the case, I fail to understand what you have to discuss with Nero Wolfe. It seems you are comfortable with your decision regarding the death."

"I am concerned that Mr. Wolfe might be interfering with a police investigation."

"I was unaware that any sort of police investigation into Mulgrew's death is in progress."

Blankenship's sigh was loud enough that it came over the wire. "Mr. Goodwin, I warn you—and by extension, Nero Wolfe—that despite the fame that both of you possess, I will act decisively if I feel the authority of my police department is being superseded."

"That is quite a speech, Chief. I will convey your feelings to Mr. Wolfe. Is there anything else?"

"Nothing else, sir. Good-bye."

I went up to Wolfe's room and found him reading his book, having gone through both newspapers, which lay neatly folded on a bedside table. "I just got off the telephone with both Miss Padgett of the *Trumpet* and Chief Blankenship of the local constabulary. They each seem interested in talking to you."

"Pfui. What would be gained by such interactions at this point?"

"That is essentially what I told them," I said, repeating each of my conversations.

"Satisfactory. I will doubtless meet them eventually."

CHAPTER 29

After lunch, Wolfe repaired to the kitchen, with sleeves rolled up and donning the oversized apron he, or perhaps Fritz, had the foresight to pack. There, with my mother as his second-in-command, he undertook the preparations for our dinner.

Saul and I watched with amusement from the doorway, but after a couple of minutes, I suggested we take a drive. "We will only be in the way here," I said.

"Not that it will help much, if at all," I told him as we pulled out of the driveway in the convertible, "but I'll show you a few of the places of interest in our investigation, if indeed Wolfe is ever going to start doing some investigating."

"The funny thing is, he never uttered a single word about the case on our trip down here," Saul said. "I am still surprised that he made the trek at all, especially as there's no client, ergo, no fee."

"Yeah, that's a puzzler, all right. What did he say when he decided to leave the brownstone?"

"I was typing up some of his correspondence as he came down from the plant rooms in the morning, settled in behind his desk, and said, 'Archie's mother called, and thinks I need to go down to Ohio and help with an investigation of his.'

"'Is that right?' I said to him. 'You of course turned her down. You surely are not about to travel.' He didn't respond until about an hour later. When he said, 'How would you feel about driving me to Ohio?'

"I damned near fell off my chair . . . er, *your* chair, and after I recovered from the shock, I told him that I could be ready any time he was, and a few hours later, we were off. I knew damned well that he would be one nervous passenger. Based on my occasional glances in the rearview mirror, I think that he kept his eyes closed for at least half the trip, which was too bad. There's some picturesque country along the way, especially in the Pennsylvania mountains."

"I don't think Wolfe is high on picturesque country, unless it's in a book of photographs. Back to the business at hand: that big old house coming up on the right is where Logan Mulgrew lived," I told Saul.

"Dreary comes to mind," he said. "It looks like an ideal place to set a movie murder."

"Doesn't it, though? And it's possible that two murders took place inside—Mulgrew's wife and the man himself." I proceeded to tell Saul what had been said about the possibility of Sylvia Mulgrew having been poisoned by her husband—or her caregiver.

"You grew up in this burg, Archie. Do you remember anything like this ever happening during the years of your callow youth?"

"Callow, eh? I'll have to look that one up; knowing you, I suppose it's some sort of an insult. But the answer to your question is no, I can't remember a single murder in the county in my growing-up years. The closest thing was when a farmer whose name I've long forgotten came home and found his wife in bed with another man and chased him out of the house, firing at him with a shotgun. The story I heard from classmates was that the unwelcome guest ended up picking shotgun pellets out of his rear for weeks."

"Serves him right," Saul said. "I wonder how the farmer treated his wife."

"There was plenty of speculation about that, too, but apparently he didn't beat her. She showed up in town just a few days later with no apparent marks on her."

"Did she have to wear a red 'A' on her clothes?"

"Huh?"

"You should read *The Scarlet Letter* sometime, Archie, a novel by a man named Hawthorne."

"The only Hawthorne I ever heard of was some guy whom our grade school was named after."

"Same man. Heck of a writer."

"I will have to take your word for it," I said as I turned the car around and we headed back toward town. "Have a look at that farm," I said to Saul. "Harold Mapes lives there."

"I don't know anything about farms, but it looks like a pretty nice layout."

"It is, but Mapes and his wife are just the tenants, not the owners. Mulgrew foreclosed on him when he couldn't keep up the loan payments, and he lost his own spread, which was down the road from this one."

"The banker as Scrooge," Saul observed.

"One more poor soul who had reason to dislike Mulgrew," I said as we continued back into town.

"See that second-story window? That's the apartment where the reporter Katie Padgett lives, and after Mulgrew's death, somebody fired a shot, breaking the window. Fortunately for Katie, she wasn't in that room at the time."

"Lucky for her, all right, especially given that she was writing about Mulgrew's death. Didn't that make the police chief suspicious?"

"He brushed it off as somebody getting drunk on a Saturday night and going on a toot. Even though nothing like that had happened around town in recent memory."

"He didn't think it was more than a coincidence that the shot just happened to be fired at a reporter's home?"

"You're getting a picture of a small-town police department. It makes Inspector Cramer back home look good, doesn't it?"

"I happen to think Cramer's a damned good cop, Archie," Saul said. "He just lets Nero Wolfe get under his skin too often."

"In fairness, I think this Blankenship is an okay cop, as well. But he hasn't had any experience with murder, which is what I think we're dealing with.

"On the left is Renson's Garage, where Charles Purcell works," I said, continuing in my role as tour director. "He's the one who started a bank to compete with Mulgrew."

"Who then torpedoed him by spreading rumors about the financial instability of the new bank."

"Bingo! You were listening earlier when I told you about the way Mulgrew ruined Purcell, wiped him out."

"Of course I was listening," Saul snapped. "I always listen. Don't think you're the only guy who's got good retention skills. I have a mind like a steel trap. It seems that if Mulgrew had ever been sentenced to death by a firing squad, you could probably have gotten several local volunteers to pull the collective triggers."

"No doubt, and to my thinking, someone did nominate themselves as his executioner. One more stop in town. Coming up on the right is Charlie's Tap, where yours truly and the very dour Eldon Kiefer got into a brief shoving-match-cum-fistfight in which I emerged as the victor."

"I'm proud of you, lad."

"Don't be. Kiefer looks like he'd be tough, but he isn't very good when it comes to barroom brawling. He gives away his moves, although he did land one decent punch that my shoulder can still feel."

"The evils of physical violence. Have I now seen the high spots?"

"In and near town, yes. The other principals in this drama are scattered: Donna Newman out west in Selkirk, Lester Newman down in Waverly, and Carrie Yeager in Charleston, West Virginia."

"It would be fun trying to round them all up if your boss decided to have one of his show-and-tell sessions," Saul said.

"Don't think that hasn't occurred to me. Well, let's head back to the homestead. Wolfe's planked porterhouse will soon be awaiting us."

"I've never had it in all the times I've dined at your place."

"You are in for a treat then," I told Saul. "Even though my boss relies on Fritz most of the time, I have to say that he knows his way around a kitchen himself."

CHAPTER 30

Nero Wolfe was in fine form that night. He graciously accepted our praises for his planked steak, then he launched into a treatise on the history of beef in America. "Spanish explorers introduced Longhorn cattle to this continent in 1534, and British colonists brought Devon cattle here in the 1630s," he said. "Other breeds followed—Herefords, Aberdeen Angus, Shorthorns, Ayrshire, Jersey, and Guernsey, among others."

"And presto, the steak house was one of the results!" Saul proclaimed, raising a wineglass in salute.

"That institution came into being in New York City in the mid-nineteenth century," Wolfe replied. "Its two direct ancestors were the beefsteak banquet and the chophouse. New York was the center of the beefsteak world because it was the only place in the country where diners in great numbers had the wherewithal to afford those expensive cuts."

"We really did not have that wherewithal very often," my mother put in. "Archie can probably remember some of the very few occasions when we had steak for dinner."

"And they really were few," I agreed. "One time, my father bought steaks to celebrate a sale of hogs in which he got a much better price than he had expected."

"The steak, whether T-bone, filet, rib eye, or any other fine cut, has indeed been a frequent symbol of celebration," Wolfe said. "Sports victories, postelection parties, religious rites, birthdays, all have chosen steak with which to underscore the gravity of the event."

"What are we celebrating tonight?" I posed.

"The fact that I have three New Yorkers as welcome guests in my home," my mother said. "I feel honored."

"You have honored us, madam," Wolfe said, "by providing shelter and sustenance."

"Thank you, Mr. Wolfe. And you have prepared a fine meal. Dessert will be my contribution tonight." Mom got up, went out to the kitchen, and returned soon with a fat wedge of blueberry pie à la mode for each of us.

"This is very much as Fritz prepares it," Wolfe said approvingly after taking a bite. "Have you been consorting with Mr. Brenner?"

"Do you mean in a culinary sense?" my mother asked.

"Of course."

"I suppose I should own up. On my visits to the brownstone, I have spent time in the kitchen with Fritz. He is a fine teacher."

That actually got the hint of a chuckle out of Wolfe, a rarity. "I assume such activity must go on when I am up with the orchids," he said. "A man is not always aware of what transpires in his own domicile."

After finishing dessert, the four of us retired to the living room, Wolfe easing into the wing chair that could best accommodate him and that had been my father's favorite. We had been settled for less than five minutes when the doorbell rang. My mother peered through the blinds in the front window and said, "It is our police chief. Should I let him in?"

"He has wanted to meet me. It might as well be now, if you have no objection, Mrs. Goodwin," Wolfe said.

"None whatever," she replied, going to the door and pulling it open. "Good evening, Chief Blankenship."

"Good evening, Mrs. Goodwin. I am sorry to be calling at a late hour, but I was hoping I might be able to meet Nero Wolfe."

"Come right in. As you can see, here he is."

If Blankenship was surprised at Wolfe's size, he did not show it as Mom gestured him to a chair. "This is Mr. Wolfe, and this is his associate, Mr. Panzer. May I get you some coffee?"

Blankenship nodded and considered Wolfe. "I know you by reputation, of course, and I have been impressed by your career."

Wolfe dipped his chin in response.

Blankenship cleared his throat and continued after accepting a cup of coffee from my mother. "With all your success in New York, I have to wonder what has compelled you to come to our small city."

"I believe you know the answer, sir."

"You are among those few who feel Logan Mulgrew was murdered. And as I am sure you are aware, I do not agree."

"Mr. Goodwin has made me cognizant of your position. He has also filled me in on his conversations with individuals who had reason to bear animus toward Logan Mulgrew."

"I must tell you that Mr. Goodwin has been something of a disruptive force since his arrival here," Blankenship said.

"Granted, he can be impulsive and headstrong, qualities that are either assets or liabilities, depending upon the situation," Wolfe said. "On balance, however, I prefer that he maintain his ready reflexes and quick reactions. I have found his positives to far outweigh his negatives."

"Nonetheless, he seems to have upset some people," the chief persisted.

"Has he broken any laws?"

"Not that I am aware of."

"Then let us move beyond discussing Mr. Goodwin," Wolfe said.

"That's fine with me. I am assuming you have a client who is behind your investigation into Logan Mulgrew's death. Do you care to name that individual?"

"There is no individual to name."

"Meaning there is no client?"

"You are correct, sir."

"I find that difficult to believe. If I accurately recall what I have read, you have a reputation for demanding—and getting—large fees for your work."

"I have been known to charge what I believe my services to be worth."

"Then why have you made the trip here on what appears to be a pro bono project?"

"If you are determined to find a reason, Mr. Blankenship, chalk it up to my unbridled curiosity. As Samuel Johnson wrote, 'curiosity is one of the permanent and certain characteristics of a vigorous mind.' I am afraid that must suffice as an answer to your question. I have no other."

The chief frowned. "Is there nothing I can do to talk you out of continuing what may be a fruitless investigation?"

"No, sir. If indeed my quest proves fruitless, I will have wasted my time and you will have been shown to be correct."

"May I ask what evidence you have that Mr. Mulgrew was murdered?"

"I have none, sir," Wolfe said, flipping a palm. "But like Mr. Goodwin, I have an itch that must be scratched."

"This all sounds pretty vague, and I have the general well-being of this community to consider. I am concerned that as long as you and Mr. Goodwin remain here, there will be those who feel a murderer is at large among us. And human nature being what it is, there will also be those who think they know the identity of the murderer. Fingers will get pointed, rumors will be rampant, and the town will be the worse for it."

"You have raised a valid issue, sir," Wolfe said. "We shall expedite our investigation and keep you apprised of developments."

"I am still not the least bit happy, but as long as you break no laws, there is little I can do to stop you unless I receive complaints about your behavior," Blankenship said, rising to leave. "Thank you once again for your hospitality, Mrs. Goodwin."

CHAPTER 31

After the chief left, Wolfe turned to my mother. "Mrs. Goodwin, if you will excuse us, I need to confer with Archie and Saul in my room."

"Would you like me to bring some beer up for you?" she asked.

"They can do that. We have imposed far too much upon your hospitality as it is."

"I'm not complaining in the least. It is nice to have the house full and active. As I have mentioned, my other children—and their children as well—do not come often, so this is a welcome change for me."

"Are you suggesting we behave like children?" I asked.

"No, I am not, Archie Goodwin. I have found the goings-on fascinating. That session you just had with Chief Blankenship, for instance, was an eye-opener for me, Mr. Wolfe. I believe that poor man is terribly worried that his suicide theory is about to go up in smoke."

"You are most perceptive," Wolfe said. "The chief is patently shaken and wishes we interlopers would evaporate."

"But you won't."

"No, madam, we won't. Not yet."

Saul and I pulled chairs into Wolfe's bedroom from adjoining rooms as he popped open one of the chilled beers we had brought up.

"If we were to have a gathering of the principals here—one more test of your mother's hospitality—do you two think you could round up everybody and deliver them?"

"It would be a tall order," I said, "both persuasively and logistically. That does not mean it's impossible, though."

"I agree with Archie," Saul put in. "Over the years, we've delivered a lot of people to the brownstone who didn't want to go, but we have managed to get them there without hardly ever resorting to rough stuff."

"Hardly ever?" Wolfe posed, eyebrows raised.

"Well, a few have needed some . . . *extra* incentive to visit you, but not many of them."

"Very well, then, I . . ."

Wolfe stopped in midsentence, and the reason quickly became clear to me, if not to Saul. His eyes were closed, and he began the exercise that always made my mouth dry as a desert.

"My God, is he okay?" Saul whispered. "Is he having some kind of a stroke or—"

"Maybe a stroke of genius. You don't have to whisper. Where he is now, he can't hear you," I said as we watched Wolfe pull his lips in and push them out, again and again.

"I've told you about this before, although until today, you have never seen it," I said to Saul. "It can go on for as few as several minutes and as long as almost an hour. There's nothing we can do right now but wait. The odd thing is, the lip business usually occurs first, and *then* Wolfe tells me to bring everybody together for the showdown. This time it's happened in the opposite order, which makes me think he knew one of his lip moments was coming."

"I will be damned," Saul said. "I need a drink."

"Go downstairs and get yourself a scotch. You now know where it is. I'll keep watch here."

"Hell no, I can wait." We both sat, watching Wolfe and wondering when he would rejoin us. Seventeen minutes later, he opened his eyes, blinked twice, and made a face.

"Pah, I have been a lackwit! The answer was right there in front of me, clear as crystal, yet I ignored it. You supplied a detailed road map," he said to me, "and I was blind to its explicit directions. I chastise myself for my opacity and beg you to accept an apology."

What was I going to say to that, especially because, as usual, he was so far ahead of me that I had no idea where we were going? "I think Saul and I need something liquid," I said as Wolfe reached for his beer.

"Yes, yes, get your drinks, and then we will talk," Wolfe said.

Once we were all settled, Wolfe took a deep breath, letting the air out slowly. "Archie, do you think your mother will abide our having a gathering in her living room?"

"By that, I assume you mean a gathering in which you will identify a murderer?"

"Confound it, of course that is what I mean!"

"I believe she'll abide it, to use your term, but I will find out," I replied. I went downstairs and found Mom in the kitchen cleaning up the dinner dishes.

"What can I get you, dear?" she asked, drying her hands on a towel.

"I wonder if we might be able to use the living room to . . . well—"

"To have Mr. Wolfe gather everyone and name a murderer?"

"Well, yes."

"Of course that's all right. It's a big room, which is part of the reason your father and I bought the house in the first place. I've been in Mr. Wolfe's office in the brownstone, and if that has been big enough to handle a crowd, I'm sure this will work as well."

I gave her a hug and went back up to tell Wolfe. "Very well," he said. "We will draw up the guest list."

"You're assuming we can get all the principals to show up," I said.

"Let us proceed on that assumption. As we discussed, you have been successful at this endeavor in the past."

"There's a first time for everything. But okay, let's plunge ahead."

"I'll take notes," Saul said, pulling a pad and pencil from his shirt pocket.

"We will want to invite Purcell, Mapes, Kiefer, Newman, and Carrie Yeager," I said.

"Add Miss Newman and Miss Padgett to the list as well," Wolfe put in.

"Do you really want Katie Padgett in the room?" I asked him. "As sure as we are sitting here, she will try to take over and start asking questions."

"She will *not*," Wolfe replied, leaving no room for discussion. "The police chief should be present as well, and he would be well advised to bring along a fellow officer."

"Shades of when you have Cramer and Stebbins sit in—or stand in—on your sessions back home," Saul said. "This could be like old times."

"Maybe," Wolfe replied with a shrug. "Archie, do you believe we can bring everyone together by tomorrow evening at nine o'clock?"

"I would like to say yes, but I can't guarantee it. One of them, Carrie Yeager, lives in another state, although Saul could go down and get her, and on the way back pick up Newman, who lives some miles south of town. That would leave me to pick up his granddaughter, Donna Newman. She has a place several miles west of here."

Wolfe glowered at his beer. "Use your intelligence as guided by your experience," he grumped, using more or less the same words he has thrown at me on more occasions than I can count.

"Aye, aye, boss," I replied, knowing how much Wolfe hates the b-word. Saul and I then took our drinks and left him to his beer and his book.

Downstairs in the living room, I turned to Saul. "I didn't mean to act like I was running this show, so I am not sure how you feel about going down to Charleston to pick up Miss Yeager—assuming she will allow herself to be picked up—and then getting Lester Newman on the return trip. I've got addresses and phone numbers for both of them."

"Hell, I know my role here, and I don't mind it one bit, Archie. When I call these two, I suppose I will tell them Wolfe is going to reveal the murderer of Mulgrew, right?"

"That's what I'm going to say to the people I'll be calling. The whole thing is a long shot, especially since we're asking them to show up here tomorrow night."

"What's your own plan of action?" Saul asked.

"In the morning, I'm going to telephone Katie Padgett, girl reporter, who's miffed at me right now but who may be of use to us. My immediate plan is to finish this drink and call it a night."

CHAPTER 32

After breakfast the next day, I immediately went to the phone and called the *Trumpet* office. I was put through to Katie, who was less than enthused to hear my voice. "Yes?" she said with an arctic tone.

"I thought you would be interested to know that tonight Nero Wolfe is going to reveal the murderer of Logan Mulgrew."

"Just what are you trying to pull, Archie?" she said.

"Not a thing, other than the truth. I thought you might like to be present when my boss, genius that he is, does the pulling—as in a name, out of a hat —you might say."

"Well, I already know who the killer is, as you are aware. And I assume Nero Wolfe and I have the same individual in mind."

"I cannot answer that. My boss does not let me in on his thought processes, so I don't know who he has in mind."

"I'm sorry, but I have a difficult time believing that."

"Believe it or not, as you choose. Anyway, he plans to share his thoughts tonight, here in my mother's house, at nine."

"Who else will be there?"

"Assuming they all come, everyone who has an interest in the case. They will all be invited."

"Does that include those who might be considered suspects?" Katie asked.

"It does."

"Including Carrie Yeager?"

"Do you feel she might be considered a suspect?"

That drew a dry laugh that contained no humor. "Of course."

"Then you have answered your own question. By the way, I never did ask what happened when you telephoned Donna Newman to 'smooth things over' after my less-than-successful visit with her."

"She did seem a little upset when I talked to her later that same day, but since then I think she has softened as regards any anger she had toward you."

"The reason I ask is because I feel you are in a better position than me to invite her to come here tonight. I would be happy to go out to Selkirk and pick her up."

"I'll give her a call, but I don't think you picking her up will be necessary. She does have her own car. Anything you want me to tell her about what to expect tonight—assuming she can make it?"

"Pretty much the same thing I said to you."

"In other words, she should expect Nero Wolfe to finger Carrie Yeager?"

"Those are your words, not mine. Let me know what you find out from Miss Newman of Selkirk." I then turned the telephone over to Saul, whose assignment was to call both Miss Yeager in Charleston and Lester Newman in Waverly.

"All right, Archie," he told me fifteen minutes later. "I got hold of both of them, and they are coming tonight, but it wasn't easy. The Yeager woman couldn't see the point of the 'exercise,' as she called it. She is still in that same apartment building where you visited her, and she is also still angry about the visit she had from Katie Padgett and 'some photographer,' as she put it. She said Katie was quite rude and that her questions were somewhat 'suggestive and insulting,' to use her words."

"As that 'some photographer' Carrie Yeager referred to, I would agree that Katie was aggressive in her questioning. How did you persuade her to come tonight?"

"I told her Mr. Wolfe was an eminently fair man, and that he was determined to establish once and for all the circumstances of Logan Mulgrew's death and put all rumors to rest. She seemed to like that approach."

"And what about Lester Newman?"

"He didn't want to come, either," Saul said. "He is a bitter man, as I'm sure you learned when you spent time with him. But when I told him Nero Wolfe, a famous New York detective, was going to find Mulgrew's murderer, he brightened up and said, 'By God, if he does that, I'll want to pin one of my medals on that man. Whoever killed my miserable brother-in-law deserves an award.'"

"That sounds like Newman, all right," I said.

"There's something else, Archie. As much as this old guy hated Mulgrew, he seems to hate the Yeager woman just as much. I think it would be a big mistake for me to drive them up here in the same car."

"You're right, and I should have realized that," I told him. "If you are willing to go all the way to Charleston for Carrie Yeager, I'll drive down and pick up Newman. It will be bad enough when they're in the same room here at Mom's house. Because of the distance down to West Virginia, you'll have to leave here early this afternoon."

"I don't mind, and that's new territory for me. I love driving."

"I do, too. Now I've got to be calling the rest of our audience and hope that Katie Padgett can talk Miss Newman into showing up."

I was able, with some verbal arm-twisting, to get both Charles Purcell and Harold Mapes to make an appearance tonight, but I ran into a stone wall with my old sparring partner, Eldon Kiefer. "Why in the hell should I show up for some detective's performance?" he demanded. "I'm just glad Mulgrew is dead, that miserable bastard."

I tried further to persuade Kiefer, even giving him Mom's address, but if anything, he got more hostile as the conversation went on. "Listen, Goodwin, I saw all that I ever want to of you in that bar the other night. You can go straight to hell, as far as I'm concerned. And that goes for anybody else who ever had anything to do with Logan Damned Mulgrew."

I started to tell him I never had anything to do with Mulgrew myself, but I realized I was wasting my breath on Kiefer, and we slammed down our receivers simultaneously. Not thirty seconds had passed when the telephone rang. Mom was upstairs, so I answered it.

"Archie," Katie Padgett said in a tense tone, "Donna Newman told me she would come tonight, and she is as anxious as I am to see how this all plays out, although I think I know, and so does she, exactly what will happen. I gave her the address."

"Good. Do you have a ride yourself?"

"Donna said she would pick me up, so we'll be coming together. I'll see you just before nine."

I went upstairs and gave Wolfe my report. "So Mr. Kiefer claims he won't come tonight, but for once, Archie, I will give you odds on something, rather than the other way around," he said. "Three-to-one he shows up. He cannot afford to stay away."

"I won't take the bet, in part because I hope you're right," I said. "What about the police chief?"

"Confound it, I had better speak to him. Is there a telephone on this floor?"

When I told him no, he made a face, rose, and trudged down the stairs. I found the number of the police department in the directory and made the call, handing him the receiver. I wished we were at home in New York so I could listen on another phone, but no such luck here.

"This is Nero Wolfe. I would like to speak to Chief Blankenship. Yes . . . I will wait . . . Hello, sir . . . Yes, I am telephoning from the home of Mr. Goodwin's mother . . . Yes, I . . . Pardon my interruption, sir, but I have a message for you. Tonight at nine o'clock, I will be gathering those individuals most identified with Mr. Mulgrew and his death, and I will be naming a murderer . . . Unorthodox? I suppose so, sir, and . . . Mr. Blankenship, if you please, let me finish! I am breaking no laws, nor do I intend to take any public credit for unmasking the killer of Mr. Mulgrew."

Wolfe sighed and held the phone away from his ear as Blankenship went on with what seemed to be a rant. Gradually he ran down like an alarm clock, and Wolfe began speaking:

"Sir, before you interrupted me, I was about to suggest you might like to be present here tonight. And you might also want to bring an associate . . . No, I certainly am not trying to tell you how to conduct your business; far be it from me to suggest such . . . No, sir, I will not change my mind. The evening is already planned and the invitations have been issued . . . No, sir, I do not think I am behaving in a high-handed manner. And in answer to your question, I am not representing a client in this endeavor

. . . Believe what you will, sir, but that happens to be the truth . . . Yes, nine o'clock." Wolfe handed me the receiver, which I cradled. "The man may not be an imbecile, but he certainly carries some of the traits of one."

"He is out of his depth here, as I'm sure has become obvious to you," I remarked. "Early on, he got it in his head that Mulgrew shot himself, and he can't let go of that position, thinking that he will lose face."

"We will do our best to show Mr. Blankenship the error of his ways," Wolfe said. I wanted to ask him who he was going to finger for the murder, as I still hadn't doped it out, but I decided to let him have his fun. Although he would deny it, Wolfe loves to orchestrate these revelatory evenings with a flair for the dramatic.

CHAPTER 33

After lunch, Saul Panzer hopped into the Heron and steered it south. Destination: Charleston, capital of West Virginia, where he would pick up Carrie Yeager—so we hoped—and bring her to our cozy little gathering.

As Wolfe would want to drink beer during the evening, he charged me with ensuring that a variety of beverages would also be available for our guests. To my surprise, Mom really did have quite a variety of liquor in the house. "As you know, I'm not much of a drinker myself, Archie," she said, "but I like to keep alcohol on hand for guests. It often seems unnecessary, though, because most of the people who do stop by or come over for church meetings don't do much if any drinking, either. After all, I don't run with what might be called 'a fast crowd.'"

"Well, your stocking up has come in handy this time," I told her. "You have just saved me a visit to the state liquor store. And by the way, Saul gave a thumbs-up to your scotch."

My next task was to call Lester Newman and tell him I was the one who would be driving him north. "Oh, so now I'll be riding with a major, will I?" Newman said. "Do I have to salute when I climb into your car?"

"Of course not," I told him, laughing. "Besides, as you know, it's been years since I held that rank. And you are the real war hero, not me. I just pushed papers around in Washington," I told him, purposely degrading my role. That was the right thing to say. Newman muttered something like "I was just doing my duty," but he clearly was pleased.

After counting the number of people who were expected, including Eldon Kiefer, I went about gathering chairs from around the house. Wolfe would sit in my father's big wingback chair, which was barely big enough to accommodate him, with an end table at hand for his beer. Mom watched over the process like a mother hen, suggesting that I allow more space between the seats. "You don't want people to feel cramped," she said. "There is plenty of space in here. As I said before, this big living room was one of the reasons your father and I decided to buy the farm and its house all those years ago."

"It seemed bigger when I was a kid," I said. "But then, everything did."

"I still feel that it's plenty large, Archie. And don't worry—once they all get seated tonight, I will make myself scarce."

"No need for that, Mom. After all, this *is* your house."

"I know, but I wouldn't want Mr. Wolfe to think I was eavesdropping on his show."

"And that's just what it is—a show. A very good show, no question, and one he has perfected over the years, although he would object to that term to describe it. It's just about time for me to pick up Mr. Newman. If you can put the liquor bottles, glasses, and something with ice in it on that small side table in the living room, that would be fine, if you don't mind."

"I don't mind one bit," my mother said, "although I'll be surprised if many, if any, of the guests will want a drink."

"I agree, but at least we're prepared. I'm off to Waverly."

The drive back north with Lester Newman was uneventful, other than his intermittent railing at "that damned caregiver" Carrie Yeager. It would be interesting to watch his reaction when he saw her in the same room with him. We got back to the house an hour before Wolfe was scheduled to begin, and Saul had not yet arrived from Charleston with Miss Yeager.

I settled Newman in one of the living room chairs and asked if he wanted a drink, getting a shake of the head in response. "Now tell me, who all's going to be here tonight?" he asked.

"I'm not completely sure," I said, dodging his question, "although whoever shows up will have had some connection with Logan Mulgrew."

"And just where do I fit into all this, Major?" the old soldier asked, folding his arms across his chest. "Does your Mr. Wolfe think that I bumped off that lowlife Mulgrew?"

"I really don't know, because he doesn't share his thoughts with me."

"Well, I can tell you right now that if I'd had the chance, I'd have killed the bastard and that so-called caregiver of my sister's, too."

That comment intensified my decision to keep an eye out for Saul Panzer's arrival with Carrie Yeager. No need for early fireworks; there might be enough of them later. When they arrived, which I figured would happen soon, I would usher Saul and his passenger in through the kitchen door and put the young lady on ice for a while.

Sure enough, about ten minutes later, the Heron pulled into

the driveway and came to a stop in back of the house. Saul, playing the chauffeur role to the hilt, detoured around the front of the car and pulled open the passenger-side door, bowing ever so slightly as Carrie Yeager stepped out, looking crisp in a summery yellow dress and white pumps.

I opened the kitchen door and beckoned them in. Carrie started for the door and froze when she saw me. "You, you're the . . . the photographer who came with that newspaper woman! What are you doing here?"

"It is true confession time," I told her. "My name is Archie Goodwin. I am a New York private investigator in the employ of Nero Wolfe, who will be speaking tonight about the death of Logan Mulgrew. And for the record, this is my mother's house, the place where I grew up."

As I was speaking, the young woman's facial features ranged from disbelief, to anger, to what I would call desperation. "I want to get out of here right now, Mr. Panzer!" she said to Saul. "Or are you a detective, too?"

He nodded somberly. "Yes, ma'am, I am."

"I've come to be framed!" she almost shouted. "And here I thought this was going to be a meeting where the death of Logan would be explained."

"That is exactly what's going to happen," I told her.

"Then why am I the only one here?"

"You won't be, I assure you of that. You just happen to be an early arrival. There will be a roomful; now come on in." Carrie reluctantly allowed herself to be led into the kitchen, where she was greeted by my mother, who knew to keep her out of the living room until she got a signal from me or Saul.

"Hello, I'm Marjorie Goodwin, and I just brewed a pot of tea. May I pour you a cup?" Mom said, holding out a hand, which Carrie took warily.

"Uh . . . yes, yes, thank you," our guest said, sitting in the chair at the kitchen table that was offered to her. The young woman had been thrown off by circumstances, but my mother's soothing welcome seemed to calm her, at least for the moment. Saul and I left them and went to the living room to prepare for the onslaught.

Saul went over to Lester Newman and introduced himself. "Jewish, huh?" Newman said, and Saul nodded.

"Well, that's just fine by me. When I left Ohio to go off to war, I had never even laid eyes on a Jew, to my knowledge. But when I met one on the battlefield, he was a damned good one. He was a field first sergeant named Horowitz, from Brooklyn, I think it was. And he died a hero on that awful damned beach at Anzio. Are you from Brooklyn?"

"In fact, I am, and there have been several Horowitz families in our neighborhood, but I think I just might know the one who got killed. The Mrs. Horowitz I knew of was a Gold Star Mother, and she had one of those red-and-white banners in her window with a gold star in the middle, you know the ones."

Newman, whom Saul had seated in the back row of chairs, nodded grimly. "Yeah, those banners meant somebody in that house had died in the war." Just then, the doorbell rang. The parade was about to begin.

I played doorman and found myself looking at the ramrod-straight figure of Chief Thomas Blankenship, in uniform, along with a slightly shorter and younger cop with a mustache whom the chief introduced as Sergeant Macready.

"Okay, where is Nero Wolfe?" Blankenship demanded, once inside. "I have to tell you, Goodwin, that I do not like this setup one bit, although I have found that it's fruitless talking to you. I'll save my comments for Mr. Wolfe." Then, seeing Newman alone among the array of chairs, he said, "Hello. I don't believe that we have met. I'm Police Chief Blankenship."

"Name's Lester Newman, from down in Waverly," the old man said as he remained seated. It was clear the chief was curious about Newman's presence, but he said nothing.

"And who's that?" Blankenship snapped, jabbing a thumb in Saul's direction.

"That is Saul Panzer," I answered, "who like me is a private detective from New York and an associate of Mr. Wolfe."

The bell rang again, and I opened the door to Harold Mapes and, just behind him, Charles Purcell. They each stepped in and looked around, both slightly startled to see two uniformed members of the law standing in the far corner. But neither Mapes nor Purcell questioned their presence as I introduced the pair to Newman and to the cops.

Saul, who knew where Wolfe wanted everyone to be seated, steered the new arrivals to a pair of seats in the front row, facing the wingback chair where Wolfe would be. They took their places without complaint, looking somewhat puzzled, as if wondering what to expect. Or maybe, one of them was simply a very good actor.

The doorbell again. This time it was Katie Padgett and Donna Newman, the former all smiles and the latter frowning. "Good evening, ladies," I said as I ushered them in. Once again, I made introductions and was interested to see that neither of them seemed fazed in the least at the cops' presence.

"Why is that newspaper reporter here?" Blankenship demanded.

"Mr. Wolfe invited her," I said. "You can ask him the reason when he comes in, which will be shortly."

At that point, I went to the kitchen, where my mother and

Carrie Yeager were having tea. "It's showtime," I told the young woman and escorted her to the living room, where her appearance was met with raised eyebrows, frowns, and a growl from Lester Newman.

Everyone was now in place: Purcell, Mapes, Katie Padgett, and Carrie Yeager in the front row; the Newmans in the back row, along with an empty chair for Eldon Kiefer, whom Wolfe seemed sure would show up. The police chose to remain standing in the rear of the room, much like Cramer and Stebbins do when we have sessions like this back at the brownstone in New York. I nodded to Saul, who went upstairs to summon Wolfe as Harold Mapes complained, asking, "How long do we have to sit here waiting for this guy?"

"'This guy' has arrived, sir," Nero Wolfe replied, walking in and easing himself into the wingback chair. "I am going to have a beer, would anyone else like something to drink?"

"I didn't realize this was to be a social occasion," Purcell said as Saul placed a tray with two bottles of beer and a chilled stein on the end table next to Wolfe.

"If no one objects, I've changed my mind and would like a scotch and water," Lester Newman said, looking around at the others, none of whom seemed interested in a libation. I gave the scotch to Newman, who grinned and said, "Thanks, Major, I have always wanted to be served by an officer."

Wolfe took a healthy drink of beer and surveyed his audience, referring to each of them by name. "Now I—"

"What are the police doing here," interrupted Harold Mapes. "May we assume that someone is going to get arrested?"

"If you please, Mr. Mapes," Wolfe said, leaning forward, palms down on the arms of his chair. "Mr. Blankenship and his associate are present at my invitation, and their services may or may not be required. Now if I may continue, I would—"

Damned if Wolfe didn't get interrupted again, this time by the front bell. Saul did the doorman duties and in walked none other than Eldon Kiefer, wearing a checked shirt with its sleeves rolled up and the same surly expression as when we mixed it up in Charlie's Tap.

"Good evening, Mr. Kiefer," Wolfe said. "Please take that empty chair."

"I don't know why in the hell I'm here," he groused. "Are you going to make some sort of big pronouncement about Mulgrew like I was told?"

"I plan to discuss the death of Mr. Mulgrew and the reasons for my conclusion. Would you like something to drink?"

"No thanks," Kiefer replied, waving the idea away. "No—wait. I'll have a bourbon on the rocks. Then I'll shut up and listen."

"Very well," Wolfe said as Saul filled Kiefer's drink order. "This will take some time, and I appreciate everyone's patience."

CHAPTER 34

As Wolfe surveyed the gathering, I was surprised at how attentive everyone appeared to be. When he staged these kinds of evenings back home, members of the audience would often behave like fans at a hockey game in Madison Square Garden when the Rangers were getting shellacked. But tonight, there was no overt grumbling or groans after Wolfe's entry. It must have something to do with the makeup of midwesterners.

"If you all will kindly bear with me, I wish to proceed in an orderly fashion, which will mean beginning by stating the obvious," Wolfe said. "Logan Mulgrew was not well liked from what I have ascertained, although I never met the man."

"Count your blessings on that score!" Harold Mapes said, to the accompaniment of laughter and an "amen" from Kiefer.

"Indeed," Wolfe replied with the hint of a smile. "Many of you here had reason to feel rancor toward Mr. Mulgrew, and for a variety of reasons. Let us begin with you, Mr. Purcell. A number of years ago, you started a bank in this community to compete with the well-entrenched Mulgrew financial institution, Farmer's State Bank. Mr. Mulgrew did not take kindly to what he viewed as unwelcome competition, and he used questionable means to subvert your intentions."

"Questionable, hah—he was an out-and-out liar!" Purcell roared. "And you are damned right that he subverted my intentions. He spread—and very effectively, I might add—the rumor that we were undercapitalized. The result: potential depositors shied away from banking with us, and those who had already put money with us closed their accounts out of fear. That man was an evil force, make no mistake about it. When I learned of his death, I cheered, inwardly at least." Apparently exhausted by the tirade, Purcell slumped in his chair.

"Just so," Wolfe said. "You, sir, had every reason to want Logan Mulgrew punished, perhaps even killed. Is that not so?"

"Now, wait a minute," Purcell said, holding up a palm. "I never laid a hand on that miserable bastard, although don't think that it hadn't occurred to me." As Purcell talked, my glance went to Carrie Yeager, whose expression indicated she was appalled by what she was hearing.

Wolfe turned his attention to Harold Mapes, who was staring at his lap. "Mr. Mapes, you also had reason to dislike Mr. Mulgrew."

"Dislike isn't a strong enough word," the farmer said, shaking his head. "He foreclosed on me a lot faster than he needed to. I'd had one bad season and just could not meet the payments to his damned bank."

"Had he foreclosed on other farms in the area?"

"At least one or two that I knew of," Mapes said, turning to Purcell. "Charles, I know that if you had still been running your bank, you wouldn't have wiped me out."

"You're right about that, Harold."

"Anyway," Mapes continued, "I suppose I could be seen as a suspect in Mulgrew's death—that is, if he really was killed. The police"—he turned and looked at Blankenship—"are saying that it was suicide."

"So they are," Wolfe replied, finishing his first bottle of beer and dabbing his lips with a handkerchief. "Perhaps Mr. Blankenship would like to address his position."

"Yes, I would," the town's top cop said. "Logan Mulgrew was shot with his own firearm, which had only his fingerprints on it. Some of those who worked for him at the bank said he had seemed depressed lately, very likely because of the relatively recent loss of his wife. This young woman," he said, pointing at Katie Padgett, "stirred everything up with her writing in the *Trumpet* by strongly suggesting that Mr. Mulgrew was murdered.

"Now I am in favor of a free press as much as the next person," Blankenship continued, "but I am also in favor of a responsible press, and I believe the local newspaper coverage of Logan Mulgrew's death happens to be far from what I would term responsible."

"We disagree there, Chief Blankenship," Katie Padgett said. "And if any more evidence is needed as to the veracity of my reporting, how do you explain the gunshot fired into my apartment soon after my first article about Logan Mulgrew's death appeared in the *Trumpet*?"

"I plan to discuss that gunshot in the fullness of time," Wolfe put in before Blankenship could respond. "Now I want to ask Mr. Newman about his feelings toward the dead man."

Lester Newman jerked upright when his name was called, as if he had been nodding off, which I knew was not the case because I had been watching him. "My . . . feelings . . . toward Mulgrew?"

"Yes, sir."

"He killed my sister, just as if he had stuck a knife in her. Does that answer your fool question, Mr. New York Detective? And he had help, a woman who is sitting right here in this room," Newman said, pointing a shaky finger at Carrie Yeager.

"I don't have to stay here and take this!" the object of Newman's scorn said as she stood and took a step toward the front door.

"Sit down," Wolfe told the young woman, his tone not loud, but with a cutting edge. In all the years I have worked for him, I've never figured out how he does that. He doesn't scream or yell, but his voice commands. And that voice commanded Carrie Yeager, who slipped back into her chair like one who had been slapped across the face.

"Now, Mr. Newman, please continue," Wolfe said. "You clearly had little if any use for the man who was your brother-in-law."

"In Sylvia's last few months, he wouldn't even let me near her, so I have no idea what kind of care she was getting—or should I say *not* getting. He and *that woman*"—he gestured toward Carrie Yeager—"were the only people who could get close to my sister, as far as I could tell."

"Did you complain to Mr. Mulgrew about your inability to see your sister?"

"For all the good it did. He told me that my visits upset Sylvia, which was total hogwash. Hell, months had gone by since I had been with her, and she didn't seem the least bit upset at that time."

"Why do you think Logan Mulgrew kept you away from her?"

"Because he was afraid that I would find out what was going on."

"You are suggesting Mr. Mulgrew and Miss Yeager were involved in a relationship?"

"You are damned right that I'm suggesting it. Word of their carryings-on was all over this town, and it got down to the little burg where I live, too. The gossipers were having themselves a field day, and it made me sick." As Newman went on, Carrie Yeager covered her face. She may have been crying, but I couldn't tell because she made no sound.

"When was the last time you saw Mr. Mulgrew?" Wolfe asked.

"I drove up here to his house, even though I don't drive much anymore, and rarely beyond the limits of my little town. No one answered the doorbell, so I went to his bank and demanded to meet him. After I cooled my heels for a half hour, he finally sat down with me in his office and told me that if I didn't stop bothering him, he would report me to the police. He called me a senile old man even though he was years older than me."

"Did Mr. Mulgrew ever complain to you about Mr. Newman?" Wolfe asked the chief.

"He did not," Blankenship said.

"How long before his death was your meeting with Mr. Mulgrew?" Wolfe posed to Newman.

"I don't know, maybe six weeks, or maybe even two months."

"Do you believe he killed himself?"

"Maybe, maybe not, but from what I've been hearing here tonight, it seems like he had plenty of enemies other than me. Now don't get me wrong. I'm not suggesting that any of the gentlemen here tonight shot him, but there probably were plenty of others in these parts who hated him as well."

Wolfe turned to Donna Newman. "You were related to the Mulgrews. How did you feel about your great-uncle and his relationship with his wife?"

She stirred in her chair. "I was directly related to Sylvia, my great-aunt, so Uncle Logan was not technically a blood relative, but I know that he was highly respected in the community."

"Despite what you have heard tonight?"

"Uncle Logan had a lot of responsibilities as the head of a local bank. I am sorry for what has happened to some people, but I know my uncle for what he was—a kind and loving man."

"Do you believe he killed himself?"

"Either that, or . . . well, I would rather not say anything else."

"Indeed? Has anyone threatened you?"

"No, not at all. Anything I might say would be my own thoughts, nothing more."

Wolfe made a face and directed his attention to Eldon Kiefer. "Would you count yourself among those who held animus toward Logan Mulgrew, sir?"

"I assume animus is a synonym for hate, which is a strong word, but in this case, hate isn't even strong enough for what I feel," Kiefer spat, sticking out his chin.

"Was your hatred, or whatever you choose to call it, toward Mr. Mulgrew such that it drove you to kill him?"

"You can't ask a question like that," Blankenship interrupted.

"We are not in a court of law, sir," Wolfe responded. "I am able to ask anything I like, although of course I cannot force a response. Mr. Kiefer, I repeat my query."

"I'm not sayin' another word," Kiefer said, folding beefy tattooed arms across his chest.

"What's this all about, Wolfe? Are you trying to force a confession out of somebody?" Blankenship demanded. "And just how did Mulgrew harm this man?"

"I will leave it to Mr. Kiefer to respond both to my questions and to yours, if he so chooses."

Kiefer sneered and turned around to look over his shoulder at the police chief. "Logan Mulgrew was an evil man, far more evil than any of you are aware."

"Does your excoriation of him have to do with his treatment of women?" Wolfe asked.

"I repeat that I have said all I'm going to say. You or these cops here can try to beat it out of me, but I am all done talking."

"Nobody is going to beat anything out of you, Mr. Kiefer; we don't operate that way and never will, at least as long as I am in charge of this department."

"Well said, Mr. Blankenship," Wolfe remarked. "Now, Miss Yeager, I have some questions for you."

CHAPTER 35

Carrie Yeager stiffened and swallowed hard, waiting for Wolfe to begin.

"You were Sylvia Mulgrew's home caregiver for an extended time before her death, I believe."

"Yes, for close to a year."

"Did you live in the Mulgrew house during this period?"

"I did."

"How did Mr. Mulgrew behave toward you?"

"I believe he was happy to have me there to take care of his wife's needs."

"Would you say she was a difficult patient?"

"Not in the least. She was a sweet woman with a cheerful disposition, despite all the discomfort she went through."

"How would you describe her mental state during your time with her?"

"Without question, she was beginning to slip into senility, which was painful for both her husband and me to watch."

"Were you charged with giving her drugs?"

"I was, and I was very careful to give her the daily dosages that had been prescribed by her doctors."

"She had a heart condition, is that correct?"

"Yes, she did, among her other ailments. But the heart issue was by far the most serious."

"Is it true that she died because of an overdose of her heart medication?"

Carrie nodded. "Sylvia—Mrs. Mulgrew—knew exactly where her medicines were kept, and I can only assume that in her confused state, she got the pills and gave herself an overdose."

"Was she in the habit of dosing herself?"

"No, and that is what I find puzzling. But she had been doing a lot of strange things recently, which I ascribe to her deteriorating mental condition."

"Where were you when she took the overdose?"

"In my room taking a short nap, as I often did in the afternoon. When I awoke, I went to check on Sylvia, and she was, she was . . . gone. The digitalis bottle was tipped over on her nightstand and several pills had slipped out. I counted them and found she had taken a strong overdose."

"Where was Mr. Mulgrew at this time?"

"I assume he was at the bank, as usual. He wasn't at home."

"Could he have entered the house when you were asleep?"

"I suppose so, although it would have been out of the ordinary for him."

"Let us get back to your relationship with Mr. Mulgrew. It has been said that the two of you spent a great deal of time together."

Carrie's face reddened. "People have dirty minds," she said.

"With his wife's condition being what it was, he needed someone to talk to, and I was available and sympathetic."

"After Mrs. Mulgrew's death, I understand you moved into separate quarters."

"Yes, an apartment in the business district. I felt that it would not look proper if I stayed in the house with Mr. Mulgrew. That would have really set the local tongues wagging, even more than was usually the case."

"Do you believe Mr. Mulgrew killed himself?"

"Yes, although I must say it surprised me. Even though I believe his wife's death, although expected, was something of a blow, he had seemed since then to adjust to the loss. He threw himself into his work at the bank."

"Were you aware that he kept a firearm in the house?"

"I was. He showed the revolver to me once."

"Why did he do that?"

"He thought it was important that I know how to use it. Because I was often alone with Mrs. Mulgrew, he was afraid of burglars, especially with the house being somewhat isolated."

"Where was the weapon kept?"

"In the drawer of a desk in one corner of the living room. It was a desk he often worked at."

"To your knowledge, did anyone else know of the existence of the revolver?"

"I really couldn't say. People from the bank on occasion came over to see Mr. Mulgrew on days when he didn't go into the office."

"Did he have a lot of visitors?"

"I can't say, because I was usually upstairs during the day, either in my room or with Mrs. Mulgrew. And in either case, our doors would have been closed and the sound doesn't carry well in that big house with its thick walls."

"What about in the evenings?"

"He really didn't have many visitors, other than his grand-niece here, who visited once or twice a month," she said, motioning toward Donna Newman. "He was always glad to see her, and she usually went upstairs to see her great-aunt, whom she was very close to."

Wolfe drew in air and exhaled with a sigh. "Miss Newman, it was most commendable of you to regularly visit your elderly relatives. That is a quality too rarely seen today among those of your generation."

"I was very close to Aunt Sylvia, and it took me a while to get over her death. I helped Uncle Logan go through her things after she was gone, and I continued to stop in to see him from time to time."

"Were you aware that he kept a gun on the premises?"

"I . . . I am not surprised to hear that. As Miss Yeager has mentioned, he had a fear of someone breaking in, especially as isolated as the house was."

"How did you feel about Miss Yeager being your aunt's caregiver?"

Donna took several seconds to respond. "I suppose she was all right, but I really wasn't sure."

"Let me refresh your memory. Did you not say at one time that she was 'off-center,' 'vague,' and 'dreamy,' and that you weren't sure you were comfortable having her look after your aunt?"

"Well, I . . . I might have said something about not really knowing her all that well," Donna said as Carrie Yeager glared in her direction.

Wolfe leaned back and interlaced his hands over his middle mound. "Mr. Blankenship, let me suggest a scenario to you: It involves two young women of approximately the same age, both of whom attended the same university at the same time. It may or may not be a coincidence that both of these women ended up in and around this community, although I have never been a great believer in coincidence. One is a teacher, the other a newspaper reporter." Katie Padgett stopped taking notes on her reporter's pad and froze, while Donna Newman began taking deep breaths.

"In the scenario I put forth, one of these women, the teacher, had the goal of avenging her beloved aunt while at the same time attempting to defame another woman, whom she believed was having an affair with her uncle.

"The newspaper reporter was out to make a name for herself with exclusive articles, and what better way than to capitalize on the death of a prominent local individual? She wrote her articles in a manner meant to arouse suspicion that the prominent person did not kill himself but rather was murdered. She was correct about the death being a murder, but purposely attempted to steer her readers toward a killer other than the real one."

"Wait just a minute!" Katie barked. "What about the shot that was fired into my apartment?"

"I will get to that shot soon," Wolfe promised. "Continuing with my scenario, Mr. Blankenship, if you have any question of these two individuals being in league, consider that in discrete conversations with my associate Mr. Goodwin, each used precisely the same compound adjective to describe Miss Yeager: 'off-center.' A character assassination was under way.

"Of course, any one of several individuals could have shot Mr. Mulgrew in his living room. Miss Yeager knew of the pistol in his desk drawer. It also is likely that his grandniece knew of its existence and could have told the reporter about it."

Donna Newman started to speak, but Wolfe cut her off. "However, in my scenario, it was Miss Newman who fired the fatal shot. It would have been easy for her to get the pistol from the drawer and shoot her great-uncle while they sat in the living room, perhaps talking. No one else would have been in the house at the time to hear the shot, as Miss Yeager had already moved into an apartment some distance away. And it would have been simple for Miss Newman to wipe her fingerprints off the gun and place it in her now dead uncle's hand."

By this time, Donna had her head buried in her hands, but she did not appear to be crying. "Why on earth would she murder her own uncle?" Blankenship demanded.

"Because she felt he had killed her beloved aunt Sylvia to pursue his interest in Carrie Yeager," Wolfe said.

"Okay, then," the cop continued, "how did the young woman figure to frame Carrie Yeager for shooting Mulgrew?"

"I will leave it to you, sir, to fill in some of the blanks. But let us assume that after she shot her great-uncle, she left the house, perhaps for only a few minutes, then drove back to find him dead in the living room. Bear in mind that this home is relatively isolated and on a large piece of property, so she probably would not have been observed coming or going. And because of the home's isolation, it also would be unlikely that a gunshot would have been heard.

"So Miss Newman comes in, sees Mr. Mulgrew dead, and calls the police. Then she and her accomplice, the newspaper reporter, begin their campaign to implicate Miss Yeager."

"Then what about that shot into Katie Padgett's apartment? Was it really someone on a Saturday night binge after getting overserved?" Harold Mapes posed.

"Simplicity itself," Wolfe said. "Donna Newman fired the shot, after telephoning Miss Padgett and warning her to stay well away from the window. Mr. Blankenship, I suggest you have someone search Miss Newman's living quarters. You may find a pistol there of the same caliber as the shell your men dug from the wall of Miss Padgett's apartment. A caliber, by the way, that you had already established as being different from the one in the pistol that dispatched Logan Mulgrew."

Blankenship seemed stunned by the unfolding of events. I almost felt sorry for the guy, but I will give him this: he recovered quickly, and as our guests—other than the three women—were buzzing about what they had just heard and seen, the chief cleared his throat and said, "Miss Padgett and Miss Newman, I would like you to accompany Sergeant Macready and me to police headquarters."

The two women rose and left quietly with the cops, Donna Newman sniffling and Katie Padgett looking stunned. The person I felt sorriest for at that moment was Lester Newman, a war hero and widower, who had to sit and watch his granddaughter get accused of murder. Our drive back to Waverly figured to be a silent one, probably similar to Saul's trip back to Charleston with Carrie Yeager, who would forever be seen by residents here as what they would brand "a loose woman."

CHAPTER 36

The trip back to the Newman residence in Waverly was indeed a quiet one, with Lester speaking barely ten sentences the entire way, most of them about how he felt that he was a failure to his family.

"You did not raise Donna, her parents did," I told him, but to no avail. As I watched the man limp into his house, I thought about how his anger had been directed at Carrie Yeager, and what a stunning turn of events he had experienced this evening.

Back at my mother's place, I went directly up to Wolfe's room, where I found him working the *New York Times* Sunday crossword puzzle—in ink, as usual. "You really got the best of me tonight," I told him. "I don't know how I could have missed those two uses of 'off-center.'"

He set down his puzzle and considered me. "Archie, I have told you many times that as one who can repeat even long conversations verbatim, you are without peer. However, you are guilty of tunnel vision. You consider every conversation in which you engage as a separate entity, without tying it to other dialogues you have been a party to."

"I stand both corrected and chagrined," I said. "All in all, you were pretty slick tonight. I do have a question, though."

"I will try to mask my surprise."

"Very funny. What impelled you to come down here and tackle this case, without a client, no less? It is hardly your modus operandi."

Wolfe leaned back after taking a sip of the beer on his nightstand. "You can credit Saul."

"Saul? You mean because he drove you down here?"

"No, because he became a burr under my saddle, to co-opt a phrase you often use to describe yourself. After you and he had a telephone conversation, he came to me and mentioned something about how you were in the midst of a difficult investigation. But it was what he said next that did it: 'I know Archie could use some help. It's too bad that he is so far away; that eliminates you from participation.'

"I do not like it when someone—even Saul Panzer, whom I esteem—makes an assumption about me. So, although taken back, I asked if he was willing to make a trip to Ohio, and of course you know the answer."

"I will be damned. And I assume that now he will drive you back home."

"We plan to leave in the morning, after breakfast, of course."

"Of course. I am going to stay an extra day to help Mom rearrange things in the house."

"She has been a most gracious hostess, although, knowing her as I do, I would have expected nothing less." I said good night to Wolfe and went down to the living room, where Saul Panzer and I had a nightcap and reviewed the recent events.

"Wolfe confirmed that you were the impetus to his making the trek here."

Saul grinned. "I admit I figured I was playing a long shot when I told him, in effect, that it was a shame you were so far away because that ruled him out of any kind of hands-on participation. It was obvious that comment got his attention."

"Very clever of you. If I were wearing a hat, I would take it off to honor you."

"As long as he continues to think that it was at least partially his idea," Saul said. "Now I just have to keep him from getting too nervous on the drive back tomorrow."

"Based on what Wolfe told me, he knows damned well that you maneuvered him into taking the trip."

"Well, however it got accomplished, at least he is here now, and he will have to endure another long ride home, which he won't relish—and neither will I."

In the morning, Wolfe had breakfast upstairs, while Saul, Mom, and I ate bacon, scrambled eggs, peaches, and banana-nut muffins in the dining room. When Wolfe came down, suitcase packed, he returned to the wing chair where he had presided the previous night.

My ever-solicitous mother was serving him coffee when the doorbell rang. It was Chief Blankenship, this time wearing civilian clothes. "I will not be staying long," he told my mother and then turned to Wolfe. "I just wanted to thank you for last night, sir."

"Please sit down," Wolfe replied. "I prefer it when those I speak to are at eye level, and I rarely talk while standing."

Blankenship took a chair facing Wolfe and thanked Mom for the cup of coffee she placed before him. "You saved me a great deal of embarrassment," the chief told Wolfe. "I don't know how the local newspaper is going to play this, as no one from there has called me yet. But when they do, I will give you full credit."

"There is no need for that, Mr. Blankenship. I prefer to remain anonymous, and I doubt very much that Miss Padgett of the *Trumpet* is in any position to report on last evening's activities."

"You are right there. Both women have been charged, Miss Newman with premeditated murder and Miss Padgett as an accessory to murder. The days ahead should be most interesting ones for both of them. By the way, Mr. Wolfe, I realize this is none of my business, but you have piqued my curiosity. I know from your reputation, which reaches down here into southern Ohio, that you charge large fees to your clients, and deservedly so, considering your success rate. Can you tell me who your client is on this case?"

Blankenship probably didn't realize Wolfe was smiling, the only clue being those deepened creases in his cheeks. "For the last time, there is no client!" he said. "I felt the need to get away from New York for a few days, and this problem presented itself to me. I regret that I can offer no other explanation."

"Well, thank you again," the chief said to Wolfe. "And thank you, too, Mrs. Goodwin. This has been quite an experience for me, and I am sure that we will see each other around town." He stood, started to touch the bill of his cap, realized he was bareheaded, and left with one of his snappy about-face moves.

An hour later, Wolfe and Saul were in the Heron with a lunch my mother had packed for them as she and I stood in the driveway and wished the pair a safe trip. Even though the car had not yet begun to roll, Wolfe already had a firm grip on the passenger strap in the back seat. As they pulled away, Mom turned to me and said, "This has been quite an adventure for me, Archie. I would not have missed it."

"I thought you handled everything very well, even if you did spoil Wolfe by catering to his every need," I told her. "For instance, he is fully capable of walking down one flight to have breakfast with us; but no, you had to deliver it to him just like Fritz Brenner does back home."

Mom started to reply when the bell rang. She pulled open the front door and Aunt Edna stepped in. "My goodness, what I have been hearing today!" she said breathlessly. "But first, I would love to meet Nero Wolfe."

"Oh dear, Edna, you just missed him," Mom said. "He went back to New York with Mr. Panzer, who you *have* met. And I am sure Mr. Wolfe would have liked to meet you as well."

"Too bad," Edna said, accepting my mother's offer of a chair in the living room and the inevitable cup of coffee. "Now, you would not believe all the stir downtown this morning—or on second thought, maybe you would. People are buzzing that Donna Newman is going to be charged with the murder of Logan Mulgrew, if she hasn't been already. And that nice young newspaper reporter, Miss Padgett, is somehow an accessory, although I have no idea why or how. I have to ask you both: Was this the doing of Nero Wolfe?"

"Mr. Wolfe worked very closely with Chief Blankenship," I told her, "but it was really the chief's case. You should feel comforted that he is heading up law enforcement here."

"My, that is interesting, especially considering that at the start Chief Blankenship seem to be positive that Logan Mulgrew's death was a suicide."

"He changed his mind," Mom said.

"Well, I am certainly glad to hear that. Archie, you know that if it wasn't for me, Logan's death would never have been investigated. I got you down here, and then you got Nero Wolfe down here. I would say we make a great team."

"You are absolutely right, Aunt Edna, and you should feel very good about that."

She grinned and rose, thanking Mom for the coffee she had barely touched. "I must be going now. Our bridge group is meeting, and I don't want to be late. I know what the subject of our conversation will be, and I will be able to contribute to the discussion."

CHAPTER 37

As of this writing, the cases against both Donna Newman and Katie Padgett are still slowly wending their way through the Ohio court system, and from the reports that I have been getting from my mother, a certain amount of sympathy has been generated for Donna, who, according to her lawyer, was defending herself against the advances of Logan Mulgrew when she shot him in self-defense. Whether this strategy is effective remains to be seen.

Katie Padgett has fared less well in the court of public opinion. She of course lost her job at the *Trumpet* immediately, and she has been seen by many in the community to be an overly ambitious schemer who misused her position on the newspaper to enhance her career. This comes from my mother, as told to her by—who else?—Aunt Edna.

Martin Chase, the hard-charging young editor of the *Trumpet*, either was fired or quit the paper after the Mulgrew episode, and following its brief flirtation with tabloid journalism, the publication has returned to being what it was before—a sober and noncontroversial community newspaper that concentrates its reporting on the activities of local schools, women's clubs, Little League games, and city council meetings, making sure to get as many local people's names as possible into its columns.

Among the unresolved elements surrounding the life and death of Logan Mulgrew are: (1) the question of whether Sylvia Mulgrew was poisoned or accidentally gave herself an overdose; (2) whether Eldon Kiefer's daughter, Becky Kiefer, had been impregnated by Logan Mulgrew, and if so, what was the result of the pregnancy; (3) what the extent of Carrie Yeager's relationship with Logan Mulgrew was; and (4) who filed the lawsuit against the *Trumpet*. My guess would be Eldon Kiefer, although it does not matter anymore, as word got around that the suit had been dropped.

As Wolfe has said on several occasions, loose ends that never get tied up often exist in many investigations, as long as the major issue gets resolved. So it was in this instance.

CHAPTER 38

My mother did come to New York in the fall as anticipated and stayed in the brownstone, as had been planned. Also as had been planned, she and Lily went on a daylong shopping excursion that must have been a success, judging by the number of bags and boxes bearing the names of major stores and fashion designers that each of them brought back.

To celebrate their successful forays into the emporia of Fifth Avenue and its adjoining arteries, I took them to dinner at Rusterman's, where the best food in Manhattan—other than at the brownstone—can be found. It was as much a success as had been the ladies' expedition to those shops the city is so well known for.

"Archie, you really have to stop me before I spend more," Mom said, laughing.

"It is completely out of my hands," I told her, palms turned up in a gesture of helplessness.

During her stay, she also spent time in the kitchen with Fritz Brenner, getting more pointers. From the first time Fritz met my mother, he has taken to her, I am happy to say. And in her successive visits, he has shared many of his culinary methods with her, pleased that she has shown so much interest and enthusiasm.

On this trip, she made detailed notes in a spiral binder as she watched him prepare flounder poached in white wine sauce, asking the occasional question, which he quickly answered with a smile. I had to wonder if she would be able to find flounder in the grocery stores of her landlocked hometown, but that would be her challenge. When I once thanked Fritz for being so gracious toward my mother, he responded: "It has been my pleasure, Archie, to have her accept and appreciate what I tell her, so different from Mr. Wolfe, who sometimes stands over me while I am at work and questions every ingredient I add as if I do not know what I am doing."

"Yes, I have been a witness to some of those gastronomic debates of yours," I said, "like the time that the two of you got into a heated argument over whether to use sage, as Wolfe prefers, or tarragon and saffron, as you favor, to season starlings."

Fritz winced at the memory, but only for a moment, then allowed himself a wry grin. "I was right, of course, and I believe Mr. Wolfe knew that but would not admit it."

"I recall there have been times when the two of you fought about food, including whether or not to use onions."

"Yes, there have been a few other occasions when there was much tension in the kitchen, Archie, but I have learned how to deal with it. You were away on a trip with Miss Rowan a few years ago when Mr. Wolfe and I had a difference of opinion, and I finally took off my apron and told him to finish making the dish himself. I then went down to my room in the basement and did not come up until morning."

"How did the meal turn out?"

"To this day, I do not know," Fritz said. "Mr. Wolfe never spoke about it, and I have never asked him, nor will I."

When the time came for Mom to end her stay with us, I took her into the office so she could say good-bye to my boss.

"Once again, thank you so much for your hospitality, Mr. Wolfe," she said. "And thank you also for keeping an eye on my son."

"He can be a trial," Wolfe deadpanned, looking up from his book.

"Oh, don't I know about that," Mom replied with a laugh. "Remember, I reared him—with help from his father, that is. Of course, there is only so much that one can do."

"You two just keep on chatting and try to pretend that I'm not here," I said as Wolfe went back to reading *The Grand Alliance*, by Winston Churchill.

By prearrangement, I telephoned my favorite cabbie, Herb Aronson, so that he could take us up to Grand Central Terminal, where my mother would begin her two-train voyage home. Right on time, Herb pulled his Yellow cab up in front of the brownstone and grinned, cheerful as sunshine itself, when we came down the steps.

"So nice to see you again, Mr. Aronson," my mother said as she climbed in. "Your cab is every bit as clean as I remember it from my last visit."

"Good to see you, too, Mrs. Goodwin. Has this guy been treating you well?" he asked, jabbing a thumb in my direction as he pulled away and went west to Ninth Avenue and then north to Forty-Second Street.

"My yes, and I must tell you that he has spoiled me. Many fine meals have put the pounds on. And I've spent far too much money as well, shopping with Miss Rowan."

"Ah yes, Lily is as fine a guide to the good life in New York as you are likely to find here," Herb said. "I have had the privilege of driving her and Archie far too many times to count, and they are always headed someplace interesting—hockey games at the Garden, Rusterman's, a Broadway show, the opera, or the Churchill Hotel, where it is rumored that they cut quite a figure on the dance floor. That is only a rumor, of course."

"Of course," my mother said. "And I know that Archie is far too modest to brag about his skill as a dancer."

"Right," Herb said with a wink. "Look at this traffic," he grumbled. "It seems to get worse every day. I'll bet you will be glad to get back to the peace and quiet of your small town in Ohio."

"It isn't always so peaceful and quiet," Mom said. "Ask Archie about that sometime."

"I will," Herb said as we circled the final block of our ride and pulled up at the Forty-Second Street entrance to Grand Central. When we walked into the vaulted hall of that big station, I spotted a redcap, slipped him a dollar, and got him to take Mom's luggage, which had been bulked up with all her purchases. As we walked along the platform to the waiting train in the dark tunnel far below street level, I hugged her and told her to "Give Aunt Edna my very best."

"I will, and while I am at it, I might just invite her over for tea and some sandwiches."

"You do that, and she probably will bring you up to date on all those local intrigues that you aren't even aware of."

"On second thought, I may not extend that invitation after all," Mom said with an impish smile, boarding her coach and turning back to blow me a kiss.

AUTHOR'S NOTE

In his Nero Wolfe stories, Rex Stout offered only a smattering of clues as to Archie Goodwin's life before he moved to New York and eventually joined forces with Nero Wolfe. We know that Archie was reared in Ohio, possibly in Chillicothe or Canton, had three or maybe four siblings, and, in his own words, in the Stout novella *Fourth of July Picnic* (from the collection *And Four to Go*), "attended public high school, pretty good at geometry and football, graduated with honor but no honors. Went to college two weeks, decided it was childish . . ."

We also know Archie's father was named either James Arner or Titus and that his mother's maiden name was Leslie. And we know from Stout's writing that Archie's mother had visited him in Manhattan and that she had met Nero Wolfe.

Taking these and a few other random mentions in the Stout books of Archie's early years, I stitched together a partial backstory for Archie in this narrative, which is set at least a decade beyond the midpoint of the twentieth century. This becomes the final story in what has become, without my intending it, an "Archie Trilogy," the other two volumes being *Archie Meets Nero Wolfe* and *Archie in the Crosshairs*.

Among the works that were helpful in gaining insight into Rex Stout's body of work regarding Nero Wolfe and Archie Goodwin were: *Nero Wolfe of West Thirty-Fifth Street*, by William S. Baring-Gould (New York: Viking Press, 1969); *The Nero Wolfe Cookbook*, by Rex Stout and the Editors of Viking Press (New York: Viking Penguin, 1973); *The Brownstone House of Nero Wolfe*, by Ken Darby as told by Archie Goodwin (New York: Little Brown & Co., 1983); and *Rex Stout, a Biography*, by John McAleer (New York: Little Brown & Co., 1977). The McAleer book justly won an Edgar Award in the biography category from the Mystery Writers of America.

As with all my previous Wolfe stories, I thank Rex Stout's daughter, Rebecca Bradbury, for her enduring support and friendship. My thanks also go to Otto Penzler and Charles Perry of Mysterious Press for their encouragement, to my valued agent, Martha Kaplan, and to the fine team at Open Road Integrated Media for keeping me on track regarding style, usage, and continuity.

And my most heartfelt feelings go to my wife, Janet, a girl from Ohio, no less, who took a chance on a wisecracking and cocky young newspaperman in Chicago so many decades ago.

ABOUT THE AUTHOR

Robert Goldsborough is an American author best known for continuing Rex Stout's famous Nero Wolfe series. Born in Chicago, he attended Northwestern University and upon graduation went to work for the Associated Press, beginning a lifelong career in journalism that would include long periods at the *Chicago Tribune* and *Advertising Age*. While at the *Tribune*, Goldsborough began writing mysteries in the voice of Rex Stout, the creator of iconic sleuths Nero Wolfe and Archie Goodwin. Goldsborough's first novel starring Wolfe, *Murder in E Minor* (1986), was met with acclaim from both critics and devoted fans, winning a Nero Award from the Wolfe Pack. *Archie Goes Home* is the fifteenth book in the series.

THE NERO WOLFE MYSTERIES

FROM MYSTERIOUSPRESS.COM
AND OPEN ROAD MEDIA

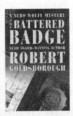

MYSTERIOUSPRESS.COM

MYSTERIOUSPRESS.COM

Otto Penzler, owner of the Mysterious Bookshop in Manhattan, founded the Mysterious Press in 1975. Penzler quickly became known for his outstanding selection of mystery, crime, and suspense books, both from his imprint and in his store. The imprint was devoted to printing the best books in these genres, using fine paper and top dust-jacket artists, as well as offering many limited, signed editions.

Now the Mysterious Press has gone digital, publishing ebooks through **MysteriousPress.com**.

MysteriousPress.com offers readers essential noir and suspense fiction, hard-boiled crime novels, and the latest thrillers from both debut authors and mystery masters. Discover classics and new voices, all from one legendary source.

FIND OUT MORE AT
WWW.MYSTERIOUSPRESS.COM

FOLLOW US:
@emysteries and Facebook.com/MysteriousPressCom

MysteriousPress.com is one of a select group of publishing partners of Open Road Integrated Media, Inc.

THE MYSTERIOUS BOOKSHOP, founded in 1979, is located in Manhattan's Tribeca neighborhood. It is the oldest and largest mystery-specialty bookstore in America.

The shop stocks the finest selection of new mystery hardcovers, paperbacks, and periodicals. It also features a superb collection of signed modern first editions, rare and collectable works, and Sherlock Holmes titles. The bookshop issues a free monthly newsletter highlighting its book clubs, new releases, events, and recently acquired books.

58 Warren Street
info@mysteriousbookshop.com
(212) 587-1011
Monday through Saturday
11:00 a.m. to 7:00 p.m.

FIND OUT MORE AT:

www.mysteriousbookshop.com

FOLLOW US:

@TheMysterious and Facebook.com/MysteriousBookshop

OPEN ROAD
INTEGRATED MEDIA

Find a full list of our authors and
titles at www.openroadmedia.com

FOLLOW US
@OpenRoadMedia

EARLY BIRD BOOKS
FRESH DEALS, DELIVERED DAILY

Love to read?
Love great sales?

Get fantastic deals on
bestselling ebooks delivered
to your inbox every day!

Sign up today at
earlybirdbooks.com/book